Queen's Court

A Novel

Edward O. Phillips

Queen's Court

A Novel

Edward O. Phillips

19/10/07

Cormorant Books

**Canada Council Conseil des Arts
for the Arts du Canada**

The publisher gratefully acknowledges the support of the
Canada Council for the Arts and the Ontario Arts Council
for its publishing program. We acknowledge the financial support
of the Government of Canada through the Book Publishing
Industry Development Program (BPIDP) for our publishing activities.

Printed and bound in Canada

LIBRARY AND ARCHIVES CANADA CATALOGUING IN PUBLICATION

Phillips, Edward, 1931–
Queen's court / Edward O. Phillips.

ISBN 978-1-896332-22-2

1. Title.

PS8581.H567Q44 2007   C813'.54   C2007-900424-5

Cover design: Angel Guerra/Archetype
Text design: Tannice Goddard/Soul Oasis Networking
Cover image: Look Photography/Beateworks/Corbis
Author photo: PLB Photography
Printer: Marquis Book Printing Inc.

CORMORANT BOOKS INC.
215 SPADINA AVENUE, STUDIO 230, TORONTO, ON CANADA M5T 2C7
www.cormorantbooks.com

My nose myself I painted white
Because, you see, I'm always right.

— *Anon.*

1

For a while I could not decide whether I had a bigger crush on John Keats or Federico Garcia Lorca. Postcard-sized drawings of both poets hung in brass frames on the wall of the spare bedroom I liked to call my office. From time to time I would study the young, untroubled faces and wonder idly what might have happened had we met. In some obscure way I was relieved they were both dead, thereby cancelling the possibility of a real meeting and potential disappointment. That was before the move.

To paraphrase Emily Dickenson: "Moving is all we know of heaven, / And all we need of hell."

A number of my possessions went missing somewhere between Victoria and Montreal, among them the portraits of Keats and Lorca. Perhaps the loss was a kind of sign, or portent. Dead poets do not hold out much hope for a widow in her mid-sixties, even were she to overlook the fact that one was tubercular, the other gay.

A word or two of explanation might be in order, as I appear to be playing the tape backwards. Most Canadians in their sixties daydream of moving to Victoria, with its balmy climate and near absence of the harsher realities of winter. My late husband, Walter Bingham, had done just that; and I went along readily as both our children, his daughter and my son by earlier marriages, lived in Vancouver. The ineluctable fact remained that you can take the girl out of Montreal but you can't erase the memory of that vibrant city from the girl. I may no longer be the girl, but I never ceased to miss the place where I was born and raised.

During my married time in Victoria I managed to visit Montreal at least once a year; however, these brief sojourns only served to whet my appetite. Like a teenager nibbling on salted snacks, I wanted more. My departure for the West Coast was always tinged with ambivalence, the pull of husband and home warring with the desire to immerse myself for a few more days in that revitalising urban energy. I consoled myself with the subversive, not to say wicked idea that were I ever to become a widow I would blot my tears with a one-way ticket to Montreal.

This idea was no more than a velleity, a wish I never expected to fulfill, not unlike my modest crush on Keats and Lorca. Then Walter died, and the one link that held me in

Victoria broke loose. To be sure, Walter did not so much die as become daily more insubstantial, his reddish hair and freckled skin growing almost translucent with the passage of years. At times I felt only his skeleton prevented light from passing right through him.

Lest I sound callous, I found myself quite disoriented by Walter's death. I suppose I should jump in and affirm that I loved him. It's just that "love" is one of those four-letter words that frighten me to death, a verb of such protean imprecision that it can be bent to mean just about everything from "I think you're cute" to "I must be obeyed!" Walter and I had been married over thirty years and negotiated together the bumpy road along which lovers gradually become friends. My skin no longer tingled at the touch of his pale hand, but there was no one in the world with whom I felt more at ease.

I sold the house and called the movers. Fortunately, the new owners were decamping from an apartment in Toronto and wanted as much of the furniture as I was prepared to sell. I decided to take very little: clothing, wedding silver, china, personal effects, and my postcard drawings for chaste consideration. While the movers, burly and courteous, wrapped my possessions in what looked like sheets of newsprint, I had an ominous feeling that I might never see these things again. In part I was right, as two of the boxes went astray somewhere along the three thousand mile journey. For all I knew, John Keats and Federico Garcia Lorca may be lost on the frozen tundra, a fanciful idea, but more romantic than imagining them abandoned in a Lethbridge warehouse.

My Victoria farewells turned out to be relatively painless. Walter and I had made our western friends as a couple, and I soon learned that a widow is not unlike a single bookend. Without the matching mate, she is not much in demand. At first there had been a round of duty dinners. ("We must have poor Louise over for a meal, to get her out of the house.") But once the duty had been fulfilled, interest petered out. I have never been good at talking about baking and grand-children, and the men were of an age to feel uncomfortable at being asked by a woman why they had voted for the incumbent government. The few close friendships I had formed were with people who regularly visited the east; I knew I would see them again.

I gave a cocktail party at which most of the guests drank white wine or Perrier and nibbled on cherry tomatoes stuffed with crab or bits of broccoli dipped in curry mayonnaise. The chicken livers wrapped in bacon went largely untasted, as did the whiskey. Even though I drank scotch and got a little drunk, I managed not to blot my copybook. Only once did I veer close to the edge when asked why I was leaving Victoria. "I'm not old enough to live in Victoria," was my reply to a group my own age or younger. For the rest, the occasion passed without incident. One or two of the party guests promised to write, real letters with stamps. Others asked me to send an E-mail address the moment I had one. All of them urged me to return for a visit, the sooner the better. Even as I smiled and returned air kisses beside each ear lobe, I knew I would never come back. Did Sir Edmund Hillary climb Mount Everest a second time?

The last act I performed prior to leaving for the airport was to sprinkle Walter's ashes over the garden he had loved and where he had spent most of his retirement years. The idea had been his, a slightly tipsy suggestion made one evening after he had drunk more than his customary quota of martinis. Rather than tossing his ashes into the ocean, or scattering them from a bluff, or disposing of them in some other quixotic locale, why not use them to enrich the garden over which he had toiled so diligently. Not having a better idea of my own, I clumsily emptied the box containing the mortal remains of Walter Bingham into the rose bed, the showpiece of his entire operation. Ashes to ashes, dust to dust. Unsure of what to do with the box itself, I put it into the bin for recycling. I know Walter would have approved.

My cousin, Diana Hamilton, met me at the airport in Dorval and proceeded to take charge. Tired from the flight and the intense activity of the past weeks, I did not interfere, but stood aside while she grappled my suitcases onto a luggage trolley and wheeled them out to a waiting limousine.

"You look surprisingly well, all things considered," was her opening salvo as she air kissed me on both cheeks.

"That's reassuring. I feel like a rag, a bone, and a hank of hair — and bumsprung to boot. Were you able to get me a room at the Château Fontainebleau?"

"Of course not. You'll stay with me, until you find a place of your own."

"Oh, Diana, I don't want to impose. I have no idea what my schedule will be. Househunting is not a nine-to-five undertaking." I really would have preferred the independence of a hotel to the overpowering kindness of my cousin, but now was not the time to take issue.

"Money spent on a hotel room is money down the drain." Diana perched her compact frame on the edge of the rear seat. Even at rest she appeared poised for flight.

"Still, I hate to start off my new life being a nuisance, and I have no idea how long it will take to find a place to live."

"All the more reason for you not to fritter money away on lodgings." Diana gave her pewter-coloured bowl-cut bangs an affirmative shake.

The only way to win an argument with my cousin is to lock her in a closet, and I was resolved to start off my new life in Montreal on the right foot. Over the years Diana and I have had our ups and downs, although as we are both verbal women we cannot go for very long without speaking. Scrapping is preferable to silence any day of the week, but my determination to be accommodating remained incorruptible.

"In the meantime," she continued, "I called Beryl Burke and told her you were coming in to town to house hunt. She's the best agent in the business — and honest. She won't try to sell you a condo overlooking a mall and try to persuade you it's convenient for shopping. I suppose you'll be looking for a condo, or a co-op."

"There's a difference?"

"Yes and no. With a condo you purchase the place outright, just like buying a house. With a co-op you acquire shares in the building, almost as if it were a corporation. Also, you don't have to pay a land-transfer tax. I bought a condo, and the transfer tax almost put me into debtor's prison."

I nodded, one of those non-committal nods that signals you have been listening. Like most wealthy women, Diana knows the value of a dollar. When she sold the family house on Mayfair Crescent at the top of the Westmount Mountain, she moved down the hill to Number Three Forest Road, one of the most prestigious addresses in the city. I had visited once, before Walter died, and had to admit that for a widow with bucks it was the way to go: a living room the size of a croquet lawn, vast kitchen with dining alcove, master bedroom suite, large guest bedroom with its own bath, entrance hall, powder room, cupboards she could have sublet, and indoor parking. (Diana was temporarily between cars, hence the limo.) Of comfort there was no question, but age had not sweetened my disposition, and I felt uneasy about my cousin's propensity to meddle.

"I called Beryl Burke because she deals mostly in Westmount properties, with a few upscale listings in adjacent communities. I assume you'll settle somewhere in Westmount?"

"To tell the truth, Diana, I haven't given the matter much thought. I hope to live somewhere I can afford. Besides, with this One Island, One City movement which has been let loose, won't Westmount as we knew it as girls cease to exist? The story has made the papers west of the Rockies."

"I'm sure it has. But we have no intention of being swallowed up by what is commonly known as Greater Montreal. We will never surrender our autonomy, at least not until the Supreme Court rules that we must."

The limousine crackled with tension. On a whim I began to sing: "There'll always be a Westmount/ And Westmount will be free./ Does Westmount mean as much to you/ As Westmount means to me?"

Diana managed a frosty smile, and we lapsed into our respective thoughts for the rest of the drive. After turning off the highway and negotiating a series of narrow streets, the limousine pulled up under a *porte-cochère* where a liveried doorman dealt with the bags. A moderate drinker, Diana kept a well-stocked bar, a legacy from her father; and after my long flight I wanted a shower and a scotch, not necessarily in that order.

∽

Beryl Burke looked more a librarian than a real estate agent, at least to me. Most of the female agents I have met in the past struck me as women who were too old to turn tricks, so they drifted into real estate, *faute de mieux*. The men, most of whom wore suits, seemed less like hustlers, but *caveat emptor* nevertheless. In particular, watch out for those who shake hands with both hands.

When looking at real estate, it pays to read between the lines. "Low maintenance and convenient to stores" means there is probably no garden or parking apron. "Prestigious address in exclusive neighbourhood" translates into high taxes; "bright and sunny" suggests no curtains or Venetian blinds. And "charming view" may well turn out to be an alley onto which backs a row of poorly tended yards. Eternal vigilance is the price of not being taken for a ride.

But Beryl Burke, hair in a bun, medium-heeled pumps, high-necked écru silk blouse under a tan cardigan, suggested plain dealing. So did her manner, polite yet without deference. According to Diana, Beryl Burke's late husband had left her very well off, and the Widow Burke had elected to sell real estate instead of filling her days with golf, bridge, and volunteer work.

She came by at ten, two mornings after I had arrived, the appointment having been arranged by Diana. I was permitted one day of grace; there would be no lying in late, shopping for things I did not need, and long lunches washed down with *vin rosé*, my compromise between red and white. The leisurely lunches would one day happen, but not until I had found a place to live. Again I realized that to have the most reliable agent helping me to relocate was a boon, if only Diana's undeniable goodwill did not roll over me like a fire truck.

Diana even cooked me breakfast. Having sent her surly housekeeper into retirement after selling the big house, Diana had rediscovered the joys of privacy, of not having resident staff underfoot, lurking, listening, breathing up the air. To be sure, she was not without help. A cleaning woman came in two days a week to tend a spotless apartment and to look after laundry. Diana also had caterers on call; her cocktail and dinner parties required no more than a telephone call at one end, a cheque at the other. Such entertaining as she did was almost always in the service of a higher cause, fund-raising for arts or charity. She distrusted politics and limited her civic participation to the vote. Diana was what passed in the community for a good woman.

Dressed in denim from L.L.Bean, I climbed into Beryl Burke's Lexus SUV. The heavy gold chain Walter had given me on our thirtieth wedding anniversary suggested that, although I was dressed for gardening, I knew better. I found Beryl — we had moved at once onto a first-name basis — comfortable to be with. Her goal was to find me a condo or a co-op within my price range and preferably in Westmount. She did not want to know about my family, my preferences in decorating schemes, my hobbies. We did not speak of our being widows; neither of us claimed to have the ultimate recipe for bran muffins, gazpachio, or *crème brulée*. We each understood, without having to declare, where the other was coming from. I felt at ease, and relieved that Diana had not made good on her threat to tag along.

The first condo Beryl showed me turned out to be the kind of apartment that looks ideal on paper: three bedrooms, two bathrooms plus powder room, living room with fireplace, two balconies, and all the requisite etceteras. What the photocopied sheet did not mention was that the walls had been constructed of drywall one could have pierced with a sharp poke, or that a six foot man or woman could easily have reached up to touch the ceilings. Balconies turned out to be small concrete rectangles enclosed by frosted glass panels with all the privacy of a department store window display. A great deal of expense had been spared.

"You couldn't possibly live here," said Beryl as we pulled out of the guest parking lot holding eight cars, "but seeing it will give you an idea of what is available and offer a basis for comparison."

The next building we visited, a handsome six storey structure, fairly gleamed with the money that had gone into its recent construction. Why a ground floor apartment in such a well-engineered and ideally situated building should be selling at such a reasonable price had me puzzled; that is until we went inside. The apartment itself could not be faulted for comfort and convenience, with one tiny drawback: all the curtains had to be kept drawn at all times. Ringed by taller buildings, the front windows only a few feet from a main thoroughfare, the apartment opened itself to the world at large. Tropical fish might not mind being on constant display, but I certainly would.

My disappointment was palpable; in all other respects the condo would have suited me perfectly. How often is one satisfied with someone else's kitchen? But in order to have any natural light I would have been obliged to live a blameless life. Much worse, I would have to wear clothes at all times. Reluctantly I shook my head, and we left.

"One doesn't want to see the world through sheers," observed Beryl as we drove away. "Unfortunately the choice of apartments for sale in Westmount is limited, and your cousin assured me you did not want a duplex. She insisted you did not intend to bother with property maintenance. I have one more listing that might interest you, a former industrial building that has been converted into apartments, very successfully in my estimation. The vacancy rate is zero; apartments are soon snapped up. The big problem is price. I consider the unit I am going to show you to be overpriced, but you can decide."

It was a case of love at first sight. The apartment, quirky but congenial, boasted huge windows that flooded the space with natural light. A large living area opened onto a covered balcony with a handsome view across the local park. Three bedrooms, two bathrooms, large closets, and a sun-drenched kitchen completed the layout. The one major drawback was the price, about seventy-five thousand dollars more than I was prepared to pay.

The current owners, refugees from the Sixties with much hair and little taste, also wanted to sell the furniture. Bulky, corduroy-covered sectional pieces sat along the wall, treacherously deep and without arms to help the trapped sitter lever himself upright. The dining room table had begun life as a door. Stools and ottomans were much in evidence. Duvets covered the studio beds.

I did not want the furniture, but I did like the apartment. As we drove away, Beryl agreed to present an offer below what she thought the owners might be willing to accept. She dropped me off in front of Diana's building and promised to be in touch.

"I'm sure the apartment is quite pleasant," allowed Diana over tea, giving her bangs a toss; "but it was a laundry and dry-cleaning establishment. Not to mention the trains rattling past at all hours. For that amount of money you can certainly do better. There's a nice little one bedroom flat in this building that's just come up for sale. It has an alcove off the living room where you could put a hide-a-bed for guests. I've seen the place. It would make the perfect *pied-à-terre*."

"I don't want a *pied-à-terre*, Diana; I want a home. I do not intend to spend my time on the road. Travel is very hard work, not to say expensive. I want a place where I can breathe, and one bedroom plus alcove does not fill the bill. Excuse me. I want to go and wash up."

I escaped to my room, suddenly overwhelmed by the idea of buying a place in which I would live out the rest of my life alone. I missed Walter; and the predictable, uneventful life we had lived in Victoria seemed like a kind of enchantment from which I had been exiled. I mistrust those who mytholo-gize the past. If, as has been suggested, the past is a foreign country, it is one bristling with pockets of hostility and sprinkled with emotional landmines. Yet in contrast to the familiar terrain which had gone before, the future stretched ahead unmapped and vaguely forbidding. Not least of the obstacles was finding a place to live.

The first scotch made me feel better; the second even more better, as my son Craig used to say when a child. I was in the kitchen mixing the ingredients for the tuna melt which was to be our supper when the telephone rang. The name of Beryl Burke appeared on the display screen, and I beat out Diana in picking up the receiver.

"I have bad news about the Westmount Mansions apartment."

"You mean the former dry-cleaning establishment?"

"Precisely." Beryl went on to explain how the owners, vague except in matters financial, were prepared to come down twenty-five thousand, not a loonie more. That left the price at considerably more than I was prepared to pay and, in Beryl's estimation, far more than the condo was worth. I agreed. A slight pause followed.

"Louise, are you dead set on living in Westmount?"

"Not necessarily. I grew up here, and Diana lives in the old postal code. But, no, I'm prepared to cross the border, if I find what I want."

"Are you familiar with the apartment building known as Queen's Court?"

"Yes, isn't it the one near the Museum, on the edge of downtown?"

"That's it, the building that looks like one of the old Canadian Pacific hotels, the Chateau Laurier or the Fort Gary. This afternoon, after going back to the office, I learned of an apartment that's just about to come onto the market. An estate sale. The place belonged to a widow who lived alone. Such family as she has lives in Toronto, and the niece left a message on my machine. I called and found out that this same niece had been thinking of moving to Montreal, but her husband has just been offered one of those jobs he can't refuse. The niece now wants to sell the apartment, and has given it to me, as an exclusive, for a month. It sounds like what you want, and it's in your price range. Living room, small dining room, two bedrooms, two full bathrooms, and a kitchen that was remodelled only a few years ago. It's a popular building, so if you are interested I think we should act now.

"I'm very interested. Let's do whatever it takes."

"Would you be free to see the place tomorrow morning, if I can set it up?"

"Indeed I would. I won't go out until I hear from you."

I hung up and returned to preparing the melt when Diana bustled into the kitchen. "What did Beryl have to say?"

"The couple in the condo are sticking to their asking price."

"How tiresome of them. And to think it was once a laundry."

"Also dry-cleaning. That's higher on the food chain."

"Louise, I do wish you'd look at the apartment downstairs."

"Perhaps I will," I said as I slid the slices of toast heaped with tuna mix and grated cheddar under the grill. "Would you mind setting the table? I'd like to keep an eye on these."

I decided against telling Diana about the apartment in Queen's Court. To borrow an expression of Walter's, she would have had a shit-fit over my even considering not living in Westmount. Diana is nothing if not territorial, and I wanted to see the apartment before declaring my intention to secede.

Finding the right house or apartment is not unlike falling in love. You understand at once this is what you want, then you work backwards in a process of justification, of rationalizing the snap decision you have made on a gut feeling. I knew the second I walked through the door of the apartment in Queen's Court that I had, in a manner of speaking, come home.

To begin with, light poured in through generous windows, illuminating the generously proportioned spaces: living room, dining alcove, master bedroom with en suite bathroom, second bedroom, house bathroom with shower stall, kitchen large enough for a small table, all feeding off a spacious central hall. I have been in houses which offered less scope. As well, the apartment brimmed with attractive details found only in older buildings. Handsome mouldings surrounded the doors and windows set off by broad sills. The doors themselves were not hollow plywood rectangles but solid structures, inset with panels. Bathrooms had not been brought up to date, but still boasted the massive porcelain fixtures of an earlier era. None would ever call the kitchen state-of-the-art, but it held all the necessary appliances, including a dishwasher.

What I would have found difficult to describe was the feel of the place, a sensation of rightness that comes with putting on expensive kid gloves or a well tailored suit. Although perhaps not to everyone's liking; many would have found the place too old-style, too lacking in mod cons, the apartment fitted me like the aforementioned gloves.

Wisely, Beryl Burke said nothing and let the place sell itself. When I turned to her after a while and said, "I'll take it," her reply was, quite simply, "I think you have made the right choice."

There remained only the necessary paperwork before I became the official owner. Now I would have to tell Diana.

∽

"For heaven's sake, Louise, why on earth would you want to live downtown?"

About to point out the mixed metaphor, I decided not to let the sleeping dogs out of the bag.

"I like the apartment, and I can afford it. Both pluses I'd say."

Over mugs of tea Diana and I were sitting across from one another in her kitchen alcove, whose motif was sunflowers, a bit overwhelming for the restricted space. I had just broken the news that I intended to buy the apartment in Queen's Court, and Diana had reacted as though the building was in Ulan Bator.

"But where will you shop? You don't intend to buy a car, so you will have to take the bus." Diana uttered "bus" as though a nasty word. "Or taxis — and they're not much better. Most of the drivers don't speak English, let alone French for that matter."

"There are several local *depanneurs* where I can buy the basics, and all the major markets deliver. There is a doorman to take in packages. And I love taxis. Someone else has to dodge the potholes and rollerbladers." I blew on my tea to cool it. "You can take a lot of cabs for what it costs to run a car in the city. I like to walk. I'll manage."

"What about the library, the pool, the recreational facilities?"

I decided to face down Diana's social worker certainties with the courage of my lack of convictions. "I can join the library as an outpatient, or whatever the term. And with the new amalgamation won't the library be open to everyone? Even interlopers from other municipalities?"

Diana shook her head in irritation.

I continued. "As for the pool, nothing could get me into water frequented by children. Regardless of chlorine I don't fancy swimming in other people's pee. For the rest, if I really want to take yoga, or painting in water-colour, or Beginner's Urdu, I'll find a way."

"Before you sign next week I do wish you would consider the apartment in this building. The location is so much more convenient, not to mention the fact that we would be neighbours."

Unwittingly, Diana had just articulated my biggest reservation about moving into her building. Fond as I am of my cousin, I did not want to be under her thumb. As a houseguest I was prepared to accommodate myself to her schedule, but once resident in this building I would find both my apartment and my routine becoming extensions of her own. With the best will in the world she would invade my life, and I understood that after a while I would have to push back, and hard. I did not want to go in tandem to the hairdresser, the bank, the supermarket. I dreaded being on call for lunch, or dinner, or whenever Diana felt she needed company. (Fortunately I did not play bridge, so I would be spared the burden of resident fourth.) To live alone after a long marriage was not going to be easy, but hanging out with my cousin did not strike me as the right solution. Far better not to let the situation arise.

"I looked at the apartment yesterday afternoon," I fibbed. "Beryl arranged for me to see it. I could manage it alone, but when Craig comes to visit I want him to be comfortable. An alcove off the living room is a poor excuse for a spare room. I'll really be better off in Queen's Court."

"How will you furnish the place?"

"Cheap and cheerful. IKEA. Classified ads. The Salvation Army Store if necessary."

Diana looked as though I had suggested going to a soup kitchen for dinner. "I have some furniture in storage. I was saving it for the children, but so far no one has shown the slightest interest. There's a bedroom set, a couple of armchairs, a drop-leaf table you can put in your dining room."

"Thanks, cousin. Consider them on loan. If any of your brood really does want anything, take it back and welcome. Your things will really help me to settle in."

"Then there's that small love seat." Diana pointed at a handsome, newly upholstered piece blocking her living room window. "I brought it from the big house, but it crowds the place. You'd better take it along."

I smiled my appreciation. Beneath the bossy exterior Diana was a kind-hearted woman. I loved her for it, but I still did not want to live in her building.

I would be the first to applaud a respect for family traditions and links with preceding generations, so long as viewed through the prism of that uncommon virtue known as common sense. Diana's apartment was a case in point. In the large house (or mansion, were that word not so pretentious to North American ears) where she had grown up, the ample spaces swallowed up grandfather clocks, glass-fronted bookcases, high-backed dining room chairs with carved legs, and family portraits. In the still generous but far more contemporary space of Three Forest Road, her family furniture looked cumbersome. The specific gravity of oak, walnut, mahogany, brocade, and gilt compressed the space and constricted the rooms. Not even the reflective surface of a large mirror could lighten the effect, capturing as it did a twenty-four volume set of the *Encyclopaedia Britannica*.

Interior decoration is not morality. The road to salvation does not lie through colour swatches, curve past paint samples, fork into the menacing terrain of furniture departments, before erupting into the apotheosis of an impeccably tasteful room. But is there another colour for living room walls besides green?

Diana, being Diana, would have considered buying new furniture for her new apartment out of the question. With a large house full of perfectly good pieces, she would make do. To suggest that the money spent on refurbishing her flat flowed into the economy and helped painters, upholsterers, and cabinetmakers to pay their bills and send their children to school would have been dismissed as *Readers' Digest* economics. A pushover for the pornography of poverty, Diana sent large sums to those supposedly philanthropic organizations whose ads featured ragged children, emaciated adults, or pathetic animals. Money spent on luxuries was money wasted. Her call. *De gustibus non disputandum est*, but I did not intend to clutter my new condo with relics of the past. I do not need garnet earrings to remind me of my mother; my father lives in my head whether or not I am holding his gold pocket watch. And I would far rather give money to the busker on the street corner than to some third-world principality whose dictator lives in despotic splendour while slightly dim but high-minded aid workers are routinely raped and abused. The milk of human kindness that flows through Diana's veins has curdled in mine.

Another attractive feature of my new apartment, one that I did not mention to Diana, was that it stood vacant and ready for immediate occupancy. I hired a cleaning firm to hose the place down, eager to move in as soon as possible. I filled the days prior to leaving Diana with shopping for essentials: a coffee maker, a can opener, sheets for the double bed Diana is donating. (Her spare room held twin beds. I truly dislike single beds; one reckless move and you are on the floor.)

In the meantime I paid my dues by preparing the evening meal. I am a reliable if uneventful cook; Walter loved comfort food, so I can slap up a meat loaf in the dark. Once I came home with the deed of sale — signed, sealed, delivered — Diana resigned herself to the fact I was moving to a foreign land. Suggesting I would be eight stops away on the Sherbrooke Street bus did not allay her misgivings that I had somehow left the compound. It was typical of Diana that she suggested I continue to stay on in her apartment until my own place was well and truly habitable. Much as I appreciated her offer

I couldn't wait to move into apartment 5-D Queen's Court, even if it meant sleeping on an air mattress on the floor. At the very least, if I rolled over too abruptly I wouldn't have far to fall.

∽

Diana insisted on having a few friends in for dinner the night before I moved out. I would have preferred an early night, as I knew tomorrow promised to be a long, full day; but Diana would not be gainsaid. I remember she had a *Bon Voyage* party before I moved to Victoria. To suggest that moving perhaps a dozen blocks east hardly amounted to a major upheaval would have poured cold water on her determination to send me off in style.

The dinner party turned out to be a last-minute affair, meaning all Diana's A-list friends had previous engagements. Moving resolutely through her Rolodex, Diana cobbled together a table of six. Then she called her caterer to order an unadventurous meal of *consommé madrilène*, roast beef with Yorkshire pudding, followed by salad and trifle. To be fair, my cousin served only the choicest cuts of beef, and a generous shot of Harvey's Bristol Cream sherry went into the trifle; but the meal still suggested an upscale boarding academy for young ladies.

Not surprisingly, Diana did not have a list of single men or bachelors (a.k.a. gays) to round out a dinner party. She believed, and I agree, that we had reached the age when single women did not need to be paired off, like andirons or bookends. Still, I was sorry she hadn't invited at least one gay man, as nothing livens a dinner party like a little malice.

My heart leaped down when I learned whom she had managed to corral: the Milfords and the Carters, both couples I had met on previous visits to Montreal. Janet and Dick Milford are both on a second marriage and grimly determined to make this one work. He is her Big Dick, no joke intended; and she is his Little Woman. Small, neat, pretty, she turns to her husband in mid-conversation and says things like, "Dear, what is the name of that chocolate bar you know I like so much, the triangular one from Europe?" Big, beefy, bluff, he replies, "*Toblerone*, Dearest." He helps her on and off with her coat and interrupts when she is speaking. She smiles, a bit grimly, and waits patiently while he makes her point. She is the more intelligent but dares not let it show. I would not be surprised one day to read in the paper that she has killed her husband with an axe.

Pamela Carter is something else again. I am certain when Pamela gives blood for a test she is shocked to discover it isn't blue. Her mother married a minor British peer, a baron or a marquess, and the connection marked Pamela for life. Somewhere between fifty and the old-age pension, she wears her hair in a pageboy tucked behind her ears. She wears a plain grey skirt the way Little Orphan Annie wore a red dress. In the winter Pam tops it off with a sweater set and pearls, in the summer with a Liberty blouse and diamond bow-knot pin. When she lowers her voice into the conversation she speaks English like a foreign language. She pens letters, motors in the country, and dines at eight, or, according to Diana, whenever the smoke alarm goes off to signal dinner is now overcooked.

Reginald Carter — "Call me Reggie!" — looks like the kind of man who examines golf clubs in his underwear. He parades a kind of machismo, grinding your knuckles in a killer handshake and wearing an old necktie as belt. He is also fond, too fond, of stating he is "straight but not narrow." He is equally fond of observing that considering they don't reproduce there's a lot of them around, that is when he is not telling good-natured racist jokes, the no-offense-meant kind. "The trouble with Chinese chicks is that one hour after sex you're horny again." Pamela puts up with him, just so long as he isn't late for meals and doesn't drop the final "g" from gerunds and participles.

As a woman who already has her ideas firmly in place, Diana does not encourage the kind of conversation during which a novel point of view might be examined. After drinks and banalities about the weather we moved to table for roast beef and platitudes. The vegetables, in matching covered dishes, were handed around by the *ad hoc* maid in an ill-fitting black uniform, her hair scraped back into a bun. She reminded me of all Three Fates rolled into one.

There was a brief flurry of interest when Dick Milford and Reginald Carter both arch-conservatives, got into a wrangle over whether those with unpaid parking tickets should go to jail. They obviously dislike one another, and it took Janet Milford to suggest they were both arguing on the same side of the issue, that prison was the only answer. I chose silence. To suggest they were both a pair of rednecked nitwits might cast a pall over Diana's dinner. Pamela Carter rambled on about her dogs and how the local dog runs were being taken over by mongrels from the spca. She had pure-bred Pugs; always had, always will. But the brutes let loose in the dog runs today? Heaven forbid.

Diana sat at the head of the table, impervious to what was going on. Just so long as she hears a murmur of conversation she is content. Like people in broadcasting she fears silence. My scheme for dealing with this kind of situation is to say as little as is politely possible, which probably explains why Diana's friends find me "perfectly charming." I am good at making the small, inarticulate murmurs that telegraph attention. Nobody is the least bit interested in what I have to say, and I am here to eat, not proselytize.

Over trifle I chatted up my new apartment, concluding with an insincere invitation that they all come to visit, but only when I had enough furniture. To my relief, nobody drank the proffered coffee, although we were not spared the reasons for this denial.

Finally, it was over, and the two couples left in tiny explosions of gratitude and goodwill. But it was not over for me, as I heard Diana telling the cook to bundle up the leftovers in aluminum foil so I could have something to put into my refrigerator. I did not want to begin life at Queen's Court with an undercooked lump of protein in my fridge, so I decided to have a senior moment. Unless Diana happened to remember the leftovers while she was organizing me out of her apartment, I would not raise the issue. And if I was caught? Like Scarlett O'Hara, I would think about that tomorrow.

2

At some point during a CBC interview, the person being questioned, having emerged relatively unscathed from a life-threatening experience, is asked: "What was going through your mind as you fell off the bridge, or felt the plane begin to dive, or were taken hostage by bank robbers?" After an uncomfortable pause, the interviewee attempts to come up with a suitable sound byte, usually improvised and invariably beginning with "Well . . ." Had I been asked what went through my mind as I stood, bloody but unbowed, on the first night in the controlled chaos of my new home, I too would have been hard pressed to answer. All of which is another way of saying that the conflicting ideas and sensations invading what remained of my mind could not be tidily reduced into coherent sentences and tidy epigrams. I felt relief at finally being here, dismay over embarking on my solitary future, gratitude towards Jacques, the hugely helpful doorman, irritation at Diana with her well intentioned interference, and curiosity as to where I might telephone to have some food sent in.

I once read in a magazine, bought to wile away time waiting to see the ophthalmologist, that on a stress scale of one to ten, divorce is life's most trying experience, followed by a move. As the two experiences so often follow closely one upon the other, small wonder marital collapse is frequently rancorous. Having raided my survival kit — toothbrush, Tylenol, Talisker — for the latter, I wandered from room to room and decided that I had made a sound decision in buying the apartment. The place brimmed with the kinds of detail that reminded me of houses from my youth, mouldings around doors, picture rails, alcoves, wide windowsills, and generous closets. Sparsely furnished though it might be, the apartment was all mine. Three weeks with Diana had only served to remind me of the ancient truth that one is never less alone than when alone.

In one of the kitchen drawers I found a couple of delivery menus, happily left by the previous owner. About to ignore my hips and telephone out for barbequed chicken, fries, gravy, the works, I was surprised by a knock at my front door. At first I thought it might be pipes clanking, but the sound repeated itself, this time louder, more insistent, and not to be ignored.

I crossed my small but well proportioned entrance hall and opened the door to find a man I could only describe as a deb's delight: tall; slim; handsome in a gaunt, under-nourished way; abundant, beautifully coiffed, greying hair; natural fibres in autumn tints; and expensively maintained teeth exposed in a barracuda smile.

"I hate to bother you on the day you moved in — I'm Jonathan Barclay by the way, your neighbour across the hall — but I was wondering if I could ask you the most colossal favour."

Overwhelmed and slightly intimidated by this unexpected intrusion, I nodded obediently. "If I can."

"It's a dreadful imposition I know, but will you be here tomorrow morning, say around ten?"

"I suppose so. I hadn't thought about it."

"If you could possibly arrange it I would be eternally in your debt. I have a chair being delivered tomorrow morning and I wonder if you could let the upholsterer into my apartment, if I give you a key."

"I don't see why not. But," I did not wish to be bulldozed by my new neighbour on our first meeting, "couldn't the doorman let him in?"

"He could, but we aren't on speaking terms at the moment — the churl. Of course, if it's not convenient …" The barracuda smile did not flinch.

Not wanting to get off on the wrong foot with someone living across the hall, I pulled my face into a rictus that could have passed for a smile. "Not at all. I expect to be here, unpacking, not surprisingly."

"I can't thank you enough. Here's the key." In the palm of a hand, weighed down by a large ring organized around a gold coin, rested a key on a chain — also holding a massive medallion which, on subsequent inspection, turned out to represent St. Christopher.

"Ten o'clock then. What will I do with the key?"

"I'll pick it up." By now the smile had collapsed into an expression of slight petulance which I imagined to be habitual.

"Very well. Goodnight then."

"Goodnight — and I can't thank you enough." the smile flashed briefly as I closed the door.

While wolfing down my chicken I could not avoid a feeling of unease, a kind of nameless apprehension over my first visitor. I would never have intruded on a brand new neighbour, not even if bleeding from the eyes. I hoped a precedent had not been established.

Then digestion kicked in, and I barely had time to undress before sleep overwhelmed me. I don't think I stirred all night, but it wouldn't have mattered, as my borrowed bed was a double.

∽

In my dream I heard the telephone ringing, only to float up to consciousness and discover the ring was real. "Yes?" was the best I could muster.

"Louise? I hope I didn't wake you?"

"No, Diana, the telephone did that."

"So sorry, but I'm on my way out. I wondered if you would like me to pick you up and drive you to the supermarket. We could collect the basics — milk, bread, paper towels — that sort of thing. Then I could bring you back to the flat."

Diana's purposeful voice helped to banish the cobwebs of slumber. "That's very kind, but I'm afraid I have to wait in, at least until after ten. I promised a neighbour I'd let a delivery into his flat."

"Your neighbour? You've met the neighbours already?"

"He rang my bell last night to ask a favour. I found myself on the spot. I didn't want to be uncivil, but nor did I wish to wait in. Maybe some day I'll need a favour in return."

"What's he like?"

"Tall enough to be my father. Teeth that won't stop. Overbearing charm."

There followed a pause. "Couldn't his wife have waited in? Or is he married?"

"We didn't get that far. But if he is married I'll eat my *chapeau*."

"How so?"

"I just don't think he's the marrying kind."

"Nonsense. Every man is the marrying kind. Some of them just need to be prodded."

"And some of them are gay."

"My goodness. Do you think?"

"I don't really know. And I don't much care. Innocent until proved gay."

"How old is he?"

"Somewhere between fifty and death. I know what you are thinking, Diana, and the answer is no."

"How can you possibly know what I am thinking?"

"It's a gift bestowed on me, by an old gypsy. I think perhaps I'd better get the day underway."

"Would you like me to pick up anything for you?"

"Thanks anyway, but I'll get whatever I need at the local *depanneur*. Perhaps later in the week we could go on a shopping expedition."

"Of course. Just give me a day's notice. Will you come for dinner this evening?"

"Thanks, Diana, but I think I'll stay put and get myself organized. Tomorrow perhaps. I'll call."

I spent the morning unpacking boxes of which, in spite of my strict Victoria cull, there appeared to be a great many. Missing was the carton with my portraits of Keats and Lorca, along with a number of souvenirs Walter and I had acquired on various trips. What the hell. I could still remember Colorado without the absent geode. At half past twelve the *bergère*, upholstered in persimmon brocade and swathed in plastic, was heaved off the elevator by two surly louts who mumbled something about a flat tire on the Expressway.

I opened the door and ushered them into the Bower of Bliss. An amiable old queen I knew in Victoria used to describe certain interiors as UHF: ultra-high-fag. I could not begin to take in the sea of swags, gatherings of gilt, masses of marble, clusters of crystal, and battalions of bibelots that assailed the astonished, alliterative eye. The men put down the chair and left. I locked the door and hurried crossly from the building, ravenous for my lunch.

As I walked along Sherbrooke Street, bathed in the hazy golden light of late October, I could not resist an encroaching sense of well-being. Here I was, back in this marvellous city, with a new apartment and limitless possibilities. I passed the Montreal Museum of Fine Arts, not without a twinge of misgiving. The MMFA is like a bad conscience, its looming presence on both sides of the street a silent rebuke to how infrequently I go inside. To visit a museum, any museum, ranks high on the one-to-ten list of worthwhile activities. Over the years, during trips to Montreal, I always had high hopes of dropping in to the MMFA, if only to renew acquaintance with the permanent collection. But the days slid by, and the return flight to Victoria found me thinking I really should have made the effort. Now, however, I live only a short distance away and will become a frequent visitor. Thus resolved, I hurried past. Maybe after lunch, on my way back, I would pop in. Then again, perhaps not.

Past the Museum lay a block of shops for those with platinum credit cards. Windows displaying one or two garments in a jewel box setting would never include anything so vulgar as a price tag. One day soon, when I am well dressed, I will "do" the row, if only to reinforce my conviction that mail-order catalogues are the sensible way to shop. Dominating the next block stands the austere façade of the Ritz Hotel, a Montreal landmark, where Walter and I spent our wedding night. How long ago it seems. Once I am settled in I will invite Diana for tea at the Ritz, not my idea of a riotous time; but I know she will enjoy it.

Best of all, I kept hearing snatches of French from men and women on their way to lunch. French Canada has flair. More than just having an eye for fashion, the women in particular understand what is right for them. They dress to suit themselves, not to follow the dictates of designers desperate for attention.

As I turned down Stanley Street in search of lunch, I realized that while passing the Ritz Hotel I had thought of Walter without a pang; I felt no sense of loss or desolation. Nor was I about to indulge myself in the luxury of guilt. I had seen enough goddamn gilt in that apartment across the hall. And if Jonathan Barclay should continue to impinge I would turn Diana lose on him. The idea made me laugh out loud, causing an adolescent girl to look at me as if I were slightly dotty. She could well have been right.

I paused in front of a restaurant I did not remember from previous visits. *Chez Chantal*, with its gingham curtains and handwritten menu beside the entrance, had a welcoming mom and pop, or *maman et papa* look which, as an unaccompanied woman, I found inviting. Once inside the door it took a moment for my eyes to make the adjustment from brilliant sunshine to dim lighting. A man seated at a table in the window close to the entrance rose to his feet.

"We've got to stop meeting like this."

Surprise made me hesitate before the coin dropped. "Sean! It has to be *kismet*. I was going to give you a call this week."

"Are you alone, and if so won't you join me?"

The proffered invitation accepted, I was soon outfitted with a place setting and a glass of red wine.

"I didn't know you were in Montreal" he began after raising his glass in a toast. "I learned only recently that Walter had died, and when I tried to call you in Victoria I was told the number was no longer in use. I called Diana, but she was out. I left a message on her machine, then she left one on mine. I went to Toronto for a week meaning to call when I got back. And here you are."

In a curious way I was grateful that Sean had not mouthed the standard commonplaces of sympathy. He had never met my husband, so how could he possibly feel anything over his death. I placed my order and proceeded to fill in the blanks: my decision to relocate and how things had moved clickety-click since I arrived. Sean, who had already eaten, ordered coffee, evidently prepared to keep me company over lunch.

Sean had been an episode in my life after my first husband was killed in a driving accident. At the time I was a working mother with a small child, not every man's idea of a dream date. I had reached the point when, although I still grieved for my husband, I felt lonely. Usually when people say they are lonely it is code for wanting to get laid. I cannot deny I missed sex — my husband had been a ten in the feathers — but I really missed the company of an intelligent and interesting man. As a professor, Sean filled the bill — especially to a young woman who had not earned a university degree. (It was only after I married Walter that I went to college.)

Sean brought me back into the mainstream, sexually, intellectually, emotionally. I rejoined the Earth People, and for that alone I will be forever in his debt. But even the Garden of Eden hid a serpent; and had Eve bothered to look carefully, she might have seen the worm in the apple. As someone who had longed to go to university but had to work instead, I felt admiration verging on idolatry for anyone connected with higher education. There lay answers; there lurked truth; wisdom beckoned enticingly.

Unfortunately there also lay male chauvinism; there lurked intellectual arrogance. Rebellion did not merely beckon; it commanded. Although never a militant feminist — on my salary, who could afford to burn a bra — I still had a firm sense of my own value. Sadly I came to realize I could never marry a man who, kindly and without a trace of violence or aggression, relegated women to a lower rung on the intellectual ladder. I can no longer remember what prompted the final break-up. It must have been an accumulation of tiny slights, like zebra mussels clogging a water intake; but one day I realized "enough already" and broke off the relationship.

It was not an easy decision, but I had no doubt it was the right one. Back to square one, I missed the companionship, the sex, the affection, the stimulation, and the feeling of being one half of a pair. At the same time I understood that when Mr. Right turns into Mr. Always Right it is time to move on. When you are tallying up that emotional account book you have to realize the only person you must live with twenty-four hours a day is yourself.

Not long after my split with Sean I met Walter Bingham. He looked on women as a foreign and exotic species, but in no way inferior. Our ambassadors met as equals; the treaties tabled up benefits for both parties. I don't remember being courted in any formal or ritual way, but one day we woke up married. And now, decades later, I am the Widow Bingham lunching with her former lover in a French restaurant in downtown Montreal only a few blocks from my new co-op. There are worse ways to go.

My *rognons*, salad, *crème brulée* having been dispatched, I joined Sean, now on his third cup, for coffee. Almost more than the excellent food, I enjoyed the catching up. Some years had passed since Sean and I had done anything more than glance off one another in passing. Since the end of our affair he had married, divorced, taken early retirement from the university, and spent a year travelling around the world. I learned all this after he had professed to be curious about my own past decades. I did not dwell on the narrative but blue-pencilled the past few years into brief, declarative sentences with little rhetorical flourish. I really do not enjoy talking about myself. I already know quite a bit about the subject, and much of what happens in anybody's life is of interest only to the person involved.

"The last time we met there was a young woman in the picture. Is she still an item?"

Sean smiled. "At that last meeting, if you remember, you suggested I was going the wrong way on a one-way street. Guess what?"

"It's finito."

"Correcto. The last gasp of a frankly middle-aged man trying very hard not to act his age. I've gone back to drinking scotch, eating desserts, and even smoking the occasional cigarette. I don't much like them, but I feel I owe it to my inner adolescent. Do you have a telephone yet?"

"As a matter of fact I do. I know it is now fashionable to trash the phone company, but my telephone was installed on the day before I moved in, on time, by a dishy French-Canadian with lovely manners and a wedding ring the size of a Life Saver. Were I to smile coyly and bat my lashes, would you ask for my number?"

"Most definitely. But only after I have paid the cheque."
"Only for your own lunch. On this there is no negotiation. Your company was far better than the kidneys. A chance meeting is not a date. Separate cheques!"

On the sidewalk outside the restaurant we exchanged pleasant banalities, unwilling to end the pleasure of this encounter. In the unflattering afternoon light Sean, still lean and handsome, looked very toothsome. With the assurance he would call he took off, and I retraced my steps to Queen's Court, with a stop at a nearby *dep* for bread, milk, eggs, and a large bar of soap for the shower.

Somebody once observed that life begins at forty. What he neglected to mention was that at forty it also begins to show. After a brief nap I pulled on jeans and a T-shirt, finger-combed my hair, and vowed to unpack the remaining boxes. A quick glimpse in the bathroom mirror convinced me I hovered somewhere between comely and crone. Small matter, as I had no plans to vamp anyone, but my insouciance was momentarily shaken by the bell. I opened the door to find my neighbour Jonathan, smile firmly in place, wearing a dark blue shirt with matching tie under a blazer.

"I've come for my key and to say I can't thank you enough for letting the men into my apartment."

On the point of mentioning his chair had arrived two hours late, I reconsidered and said nothing. The key lay in a kitchen drawer, sequestered from the confusion of unpacking.

"Are you pleased with the way the chair looks?"

"Sure," he replied without much enthusiasm. "It's not my favourite colour, but the fabric was half price. Now, let me take you away from all this;" he waved his hand dismissively at the cartons, "and offer you a drink. I'm just about to pour."

"Thanks, but I really should stay put and finish unpacking. Besides, I'm hardly dressed for the cocktail hour."

"Not to worry. I'm going to change into something loose. Just for a few minutes." He held out his arm, hand extended, in a gesture reminiscent of a grade school teacher herding children into line. Were I to refuse would I be sent to the principal's office? I was beginning to suspect Jonathan Barclay was He-Who-Must-Be-Obeyed. Sooner or later I would have to deal with the situation, but perhaps now was not the moment. Obediently I followed him across the hall and into his apartment.

Less is not more; more is more. I threaded my way through a thicket of occasional chairs and tiny tables, past a truncated column holding a Roman bust, around a lectern on which rested an open dictionary, to sit in a striped wing chair shrouded by a fern on a three-legged stand.

"What will you drink? Gin? Rum? Sherry?"

"Scotch, if you have it."

"Only single malt."

"Suits me. Equal parts whiskey and water. No ice thanks." A slight pause followed while he teased a bottle of whiskey from a Chinese cabinet, clawed off the foil, and unscrewed the cap. "Funny, I didn't have you pegged as a scotch drinker."

"I gave up martinis years ago, under orders from my husband. They acted like truth serum. Apparently I stepped all over people's feelings, but I had trouble apologizing the next day, as I couldn't remember what I had said."

Jonathan laughed. "An occupational hazard for the martini drinker, but I'm going to have one anyway. First let me go and change."

Moments later, while I was still trying to absorb the glitter and clutter, Jonathan made an entrance wearing a black turtleneck over black slacks and sandals, definitely not Birkenstocks. I would have thought a joint more in keeping with the garb than a martini, but then he had not expected me to drink scotch.

"*Alley-Oop!*" I raised my glass.

"Mud in your eye! I guess we both just dated ourselves." He took a generous swallow of his martini on the rocks. "It's been a day and a half. I had an important lunch meeting and I began with the worst bad hair day on record. Have you ever had one of those days when not even the Red Cross could salvage your hair?"

"Have I not. And where are the support groups for bad hair days? Where is the funding?"

"You do understand." Jonathan crossed to sit in the new persimmon *bergère*. With his black silhouette, he cut quite a languid dash. Something told me as I sipped away at my scotch, a bit too redolent of peat for my taste, that whatever remained of my virtue was not in peril.

Fortified by my drink, I decided to short-circuit tact and cut directly to the great North American question: "So what do you do for a living?" — although I softened the edges. "Was your lunch — the bad hair lunch — a success?"

"I suppose so. I won't know for a few days."

"Was it to do with work?"

He gave his head an affirmative shake.

"May I ask what? I know it's really none of my business, but these days we seem to be defined more by what we do than by what we are."

"So true." But he was not about to be pigeonholed. "Actually I do everything and nothing. Mostly I'm a — a dealer, I suppose. I try to put people in touch with things they want to own." He laughed, laughter without mirth. "You could almost say I pimp possessions. Should you want a Quebec pine *armoire* — although why one would want a Quebec pine *armoire* escapes me — but should you be so inclined, I will try to find one for you."

I was spared having to reply by the telephone. Jonathan went to pick it up in one of the bedrooms, from which I could hear snatches of the conversation. "But you told me you'd be working late … I have someone here … Give me half to three quarters of an hour."

Suddenly I had become "*de trop*," as Diana would have said, popping the final "p" with explosive emphasis. To foster the illusion I had not overheard the conversation I edged my way over to a kind of sideboard, in oak I surmised, with shelves in which a deep groove held plates upright. The plates, soft white with a wide pink boarder edged in gold, showed, on closer inspection, a garland of flowers in the centre, most probably hand-painted, as each garland differed from the others. I have always disliked pink; the only time in my life I wore the colour was as a bridesmaid at Diana's wedding, but I had to admit the plates were handsome.

As I stood in slightly self-conscious admiration, Jonathan joined me.

"I was just admiring your plates."

"Interesting, aren't they. French — Eighteenth Century. I may have a buyer for them, if we can agree on a price."

It was then I realized, without having to be told, that everything in Jonathan's flat must be for sale. He was, quite simply, a dealer who worked out of his apartment. At once a red light began to flash inside my head. One of the strictures imposed upon the residents of Queen's Court stated that the premises were strictly residential and not to be used for any commercial purpose. I wondered whether there could be any connection between the business and the odd fact that Jonathan admitted to being on bad terms with the doorman. Now was not the time to find out, as my host had not resumed his seat. I finished my drink in one large swallow.

"That hit the spot. And now I really must run along. Until I finish my unpacking I won't know what I need to buy."

Jonathan did not urge me to stay, ushering me out of his apartment as neatly as he had urged me in. As I let myself back into my own place I realized my new neighbour was a man accustomed to "having his own way," as my mother would have said. I suspected he would require a bit of handling, as

I also suspected a petulant wilfulness lurked just below the surface.

The message light on my telephone winked invitingly, and Sean's voice came on to suggest we have dinner sometime the following week. That pleasant prospect put Jonathan right out of my mind, and I returned to my unpacking with a high heart.

⁓

I spent the next few days unpacking, settling in, and dodging Diana. Fortunately my telephone displayed the caller, and I pretended I was out when Diana's name frequently came onto the screen. When I was a child I used to play house, lining up my dolls, to whom I had just given birth, and strong-arming one of the local boys to be father. Boys were never much good at playing house; I often had to function as a single parent. Now I was playing house for real and enjoying it far more than I had as a girl. I did not need a boy as pretend husband, and the doll baby had grown up and moved out. These were enchanted days, but enchantment tends to be a transient rather than permanent state.

3

*M*y former sister-in-law, Helen Morrison, telephoned to say she had heard I was back in town and when can we get together for lunch. Hearing the gin and cigarette saturated voice on the telephone made me realize the return to Montreal was not without its drawbacks. Many years ago she had been married to Christopher, the youngest of my four brothers and by far the most interesting. He was also the smartest and the only one to go to college, paying his way with a series of scholarships supplemented by part-time jobs.

My father, whose ring-around-the-collar ought to have been red, helped out a little in spite of his professed scorn for book learning. Having graduated with pride from the School of Hard Knocks, he looked down on any kind of education that lacked immediate practical application. I suspect that much of his bluster was meant to camouflage his own lack of formal learning. Who needs literature, history, or philosophy. Commerce was the way to go. As for the professions — law, medicine, architecture — they were so far beyond his scope as to be incomprehensible.

My three older brothers were not much better, but Christopher understood that life offered more than baseball, broads, beer, and bonding. When he was awarded an IODE scholarship, even my other brothers — who treated Christopher as a kind of mascot — put pressure on Father to let him study for a B.A. I longed to attend university, like my cousin Diana and her set; but since I was a girl my chances remained zero. Business college and a secretarial job were the best I could aspire to, but I gleaned a deep, vicarious thrill from watching Christopher enroll at McGill University.

From my present perspective I can see Christopher had been almost a prototype: a gay adolescent living in an environment where nobody one knew could possibly, even remotely, be "like that." Granted, there were strange men who did nasty things to little boys, and perverts haunting public toilets and doing unpleasant things in the bushes; but they remained as foreign to my world as creatures from Mars. Mostly "they" inhabited a world of burly jokes: "Did you hear the one about the two queers ...?" Had Christopher experienced doubts about his sexuality — and how could he have not — he faced his problems alone. Even were he to have confided in me I could have offered little support or advice, so profound was my naiveté in matters sexual. In our household sex was one big dirty joke, with little hard information with which to tame the unruly hormones.

At McGill, Christopher met Helen Morrison, and they began to sit together during those lectures they shared. Helen had been one of those fecundity females, always on the verge of a period or an ovulation. She bummed cigarettes and sanitary napkins. She also ate like a man, putting away vast quantities of food with the lip-smacking relish of a drab in a Hogarth painting. Apples disappeared in great, crackling bites; watermelon juice spilled down her chin as she spat pips into her hand; oranges were stripped of their skin without benefit of a knife. Butter smeared her mouth while corn cobs piled up on her plate; two frankfurters jostled for space on a single roll; baked potatoes, their skins leaking sour cream, vanished in tandem. Thoroughly drilled in the correct use of knife and fork, she preferred to eat meat with her fingers, rolling slices of beef into cigars, brandishing lamb chops by the bone, holding slices of pork as if about to play the harmonica. She inhaled desserts.

My father loved to watch her eat, announcing he enjoyed a woman with a good appetite. His loud enthusiasm quenched my mother's quiet disapproval. The meek may inherit the earth; they also get to do the washing up.

At a time when girls gave one another Toni Home Permanents or rolled the ends of their hair in rags to obtain the perfect pageboy, Helen Morrison wore her waist length hair in a braid fastened with a rubber band. From her treadle Singer came a series of dirndl skirts, sewn from the remainder bin at Marshall's, a long-vanished fabric store, to be topped by peasant blouses with ribbons in primary colours threaded through the eyelet trim. Not for Helen the cashmere sweater sets, Black Watch skirts, or penny loafers which for many students made up the winter uniform. Helen Morrison was one of the first girls to wear opaque black stockings, scarves indoors, and skirts which fell in voluminous folds to her admittedly thick ankles. She abandoned clip-ons to have her ears pierced and wore chandelier earrings which drew almost as much attention as the large rings on her forefingers. A baker's dozen silver bangles jingled on her left arm.

She called everyone "Darling" when this appellation was still the preserve of sweethearts and bisexual actresses. Helen Morrison soon earned herself a reputation on campus for being fast, but such was her presence — a combination of height, weight, costume — that few young men dared to approach. Christopher once described her as voluptuous (voluptuous being a pit stop between well developed and fat), while I overheard my other brothers fantasizing about the opulent body beneath the layers of costume. The net result of this overpowering presence was a string of Saturday nights spent alone. Not one of the randy fraternity types, who carried a condom in the snap clasp change compartment of their bulky wallets, screwed up the courage to ask her out. Rather than risk rebuff, these testosterone-tried college louts preferred to drink beer with their own kind and boast what they would like to do with Morrison if and when they got the chance.

Christopher and Helen drifted into an affair. I know because more than once I was pressed into service as chaperone, the idea being that if a female member of the family tagged along on weekends then nothing untoward would happen. I'd bet the rent that Helen initiated the proceedings and also that Christopher was a virgin, at least as far as women were concerned.

After a while they split up, mainly because Christopher wanted to study, while Helen found herself at university *faute de mieux*. She made more demands on his time than he was prepared to allow. A row ensued, and she stormed out. Love affairs have their own ironclad rules, one of which is at least one steamy reconciliation. What I never learned for certain was whether Helen neglected to insert her diaphragm, or whether she inserted it incorrectly, or whether maybe the rings of Saturn were out of alignment; but the disquieting fact remained that she, by the onset of whose periods the Greenwich Observatory could have fine-tuned its chronometers, was late.

The defenses crumbled. Theatrical makeup, dramatic clothes, flamboyant jewellery could not conceal the fact that Helen was just another college girl in trouble. Why she chose me to confide in I'll never know, but one afternoon over coffee she blurted out the story. Although floored by the news, I urged her to give me a day or so to think things through and to decide on the best course of action. I remember trying my best to sound worldly and confident while trying to prevent my jaw from falling open in astonishment. What Helen wanted was an instant solution, which I was unable to provide. Panic stricken, she confessed everything to her parents.

What followed turned out to be as formal as a minuet. Mr. and Mrs. Morrison paid a call on my parents. The case was simple: Christopher had gotten their daughter into trouble, and now he must do the right thing. My parents agreed, just as they would have agreed on the need for keeping the death penalty, reciting the Lord's Prayer in schools, and restricting immigration. Helen was too showy for Mother's taste, but the Morrisons had money. No one would ever accuse them of being top drawer; but Mother felt she had married beneath her, and one must move with the times. Also it was evident to me that both mothers found themselves unexpectedly affected by the idea of a grandchild, while my father beamed at the idea that his slightly sissy son had knocked up a girl. Christopher and his father had a little talk, and the wedding took place two days after my brother wrote his final exam.

By then I was being courted by a sexy Slav, whom I eventually married. Naturally I began to see less of Christopher, although he did ask me to be godmother to the child when he or she was born. Then Helen slipped and fell heavily on the tiles surrounding a friend's swimming pool. She miscarried in the ambulance, moved back to her parents' house, and the marriage petered out. Ever the gentleman, Christopher agreed to be discovered in a cheap hotel room with a lady who rented by the hour. Detectives arrived, half an hour late as it turned out, and took note of Christopher and the woman clad only in her slip. They also noticed the bottle of rye from which they each had a hefty drink before leaving. The woman then suggested to Christopher, trim and blond, that, since she had already been paid for the night, he might like to have his money's worth. He declined. Helen divorced Christopher on grounds of adultery, and that was the end of that. There were mutterings of "Isn't it a shame!" and "Who would have thought?" but secretly everyone felt hugely relieved.

Helen took up marriage as a career, her second marriage ending in divorce and the third leaving her a widow. Husband number four went to prison on charges of currency fraud and insider trading. She dumped him, but I never learned whether she bothered to obtain a divorce. A woman, about whom other women love to gossip, Helen provided conversational fodder for many a lunch of spritzers and *salade niçoise*. I learned that she had prospered through her various marriages, her widow's mite expanding into a blue-chip portfolio of some dimension.

We met for lunch at *Casa Bertolini*, a recently opened restaurant that had not yet been reviewed in the local press and still tried eagerly to please. Helen had not aged well. Too many husbands, cigarettes, and mornings after had taken their toll. By now "voluptuous" had expanded into "portly," and in all the wrong places. In an attempt at camouflage, she wore layers. Gone was the gypsy fortune-teller look to be replaced by a mix and match approach where everything mixed and nothing matched. Silver and turquoise jewellery had given way to quantities of gold chains and bangles which failed to salvage *Le Look*.

We exchanged air kisses, fortunately, as I feared her heavy peach foundation would come off on my second-best black suit.

"You're looking good, Louise. Welcome back to Montreal."

"Thanks, Helen. You've changed very little, I'm glad to see." If it is a sin to tell a lie, it would have been a far greater sin to tell the truth.

A *maitre d'hôtel*, whose profile belonged on a medal, showed us to our reserved booth. The decorator had chosen canary yellow tablecloths and turquoise napkins, which fought each other for attention. At once Helen ordered a gin and tonic then asked what I wanted to kick off with. I opted for white wine.

Helen wasted no time in small talk. "What's the news of Christopher?"

"He's retired from teaching, as you probably know. He and his friend live in Stratford during the summer; they like the theatre, and they have a condo in Sarasota for the winter.

53

He's well, much the same. Hair now grey. A little thicker around the middle, but still looking ten years younger than his chronological age."

"Pity he turned gay. He was by far the most interesting of my husbands. Smart! Outside of making money, my other husbands knew zip. My second husband was the kind of man who wore a poppy in his lapel from Thanksgiving until Christmas; the third couldn't count to twenty-one without dropping his pants; and the fourth looked at every woman twice, first at her tits, then at her face. He couldn't get on with women, so he got off with them."

Our drinks arrived. Helen added a splash of tonic to her gin, then drank half in one swallow. The waiter presented menus, and Helen ordered another gin. Feeling frankly hungry, I made inroads into the bread. The waiter put down a plate with four tiny pizzas; I ate my two with relish.

"Still and all," continued Helen, "it's not much fun being alone." She paused to fish around in her capacious handbag for cigarettes and a gold lighter. "Do you mind?" She put the cigarette between her lips and flicked the lighter without waiting for an answer. "You don't have to worry about my lungs. These cigarettes have nothing but natural tars and nicotine, and I never smoke between cigarettes."

As Helen took another swig of her gin I had an ominous premonition that I was in for an "ain't-it-awful" lunch. I feared having to eat my tortellini to the melancholy refrain of

Helen presenting herself as victim. I thought of Walter and of how uncompromising he had been towards those who volunteered to be victims. Walter regarded professional victims in much the same way he would have viewed lepers, had they still roamed the streets with clapper and bell. To be sure, he did not denigrate genuine victims, those who endured fire, flood, famine, earthquakes, tidal waves, or volcanic eruptions. He read of these natural disasters with dismay and contributed generously to relief agencies, even as he realized the contribution would probably help to underwrite gold-plated fixtures in some demagogic African bathroom. The victims he disdained were those who rushed headlong towards their martyrdom: battered women coaxed from shelters by abusive men to endure further abuse, those with destroyed livers who drank heavily, or emphysema victims who smoked two packs a day. Then there stretched the whole minefield of sexual misbehaviour aired on confessional TV: the women who discovered husbands to be sleeping with stepdaughters or mothers-in-law, sometimes both at once; sad, silly, gay adolescents who came out in redneck country and were dismayed not to be applauded for their honesty; office workers who screwed around on the job, only to be outraged when reprimanded, demoted, or fired. Walter understood that most of those who campaign for sympathy remained victims of their own stupidity; and it was just this kind of victimhood, along with body piercing, day-glo hair, and rollers in the supermarket that he refused to countenance. His intransigence had rubbed off on me, and I braced myself for Helen's onslaught.

"As I was saying," she continued, "it's not a whole hell of a lot of fun being alone, but you know something? It beats the hell out of living with those dickheads I married. What was that bumper sticker? 'In order to find a prince you have to kiss a lot of toads.' Well, kiddo, in my marriages for a little bit of sex I had to put up with a whole lot of shit, sorry: faeces. I'm so much better off now I can't believe it. Let's order."

When food finally arrived Helen tucked in with the same gusto I remembered from when she was dating Christopher. Obviously the extra pounds came from somewhere; but, unlike many smokers, she did not allow cigarettes to stun her appetite. She smoked between courses.

"Thanks for holding your breath while I smoke, Louise. I know I can stop; I've done it dozens of times, but the road to good intentions is paved with hell."

"I don't smoke because I don't enjoy it. I tried when I was younger, but it didn't take. When I think of all the car exhaust, furnace fumes, industrial pollution we inhale daily, I can't get too worked up over a little cigarette smoke."

"A sensible woman. Now that I've given up sex, or vice-versa, I've got to have something. Unfortunately there's no life guard in the gene pool, and if I didn't smoke I'd be Two-Ton Tessie." Helen inhaled right down to her knees. "You know something? I miss sex a lot less than I should. What I don't miss is the before and after. Furthermore, women never suffer from premature ejaculation."

I laughed. "I guess they don't at that. Are you having coffee?"

"And spoil a perfectly good edge? You have some while I get the cheque."

With a parting bit of advice that, now I was single again, I should not date outside the species, Helen drove off in the front seat of a taxi. I could hardly blame her. Once your feet are trapped in the well behind the driver's seat, you need a crane to get yourself out. As I strolled back to my apartment I realized, to my surprise, that I had enjoyed my lunch. Far from lapsing into misery mode, as I had initially feared, Helen turned out to be surprisingly upbeat. Unlike many I have known, whom gin makes morose, she grew progressively more cheerful with each swallow. In spite of age, weight, and a pronounced smoker's wheeze, she looked the world straight in the eye and found it worth confronting.

In almost throwaway fashion she had proffered some nuggets of sound advice on being a widow. One in particular stuck in my mind; namely that as a single woman I should not look for support from married couples. This *perçu* came in the form of a riddle: What has four legs and bites its friends? Answer: A happily married couple. Thinking back on my *soi-disant* Victoria support group, most of whom had chosen to keep me at arm's length, I could not completely agree. However, I had not been a widow all that long, and such friends as I had in Montreal were mostly unattached. On balance I decided that as a friend Helen would turn out to be high-maintenance, but that did not preclude the occasional lunch.

The message light flickered on my telephone. Punching in the six-digit code, Walter's birthday, (10/11/21) I listened to a woman's voice I did not recognize. She identified herself as Beatrice Lane, niece of the woman from whom I had bought the apartment. She said she would call back, then suggested I could call her collect and gave a number.

As the afternoon was already well advanced I thought I might wait until after six, when Beatrice Lane might more likely be at home. The telephone rang at that instant, and I answered.

"Mrs. Bingham, it's Beatrice Lane again. I hope I'm not catching you at an inconvenient time."

"Not at all. I'm just in, and I only just picked up your message."

"Let me get right to the point. I was in the hospital when my aunt's apartment was sold. As a result I was unable to come to Montreal to supervise the packing and shipping. I had to rely on a friend. Some of my aunt's things are missing, and I was wondering if they might be downstairs in her locker, your locker I mean."

"They may well be, Mrs. Lane. I have to confess I haven't checked out the locker since I visited the building with the agent. I am rather underfurnished at the moment, so the problem of extra storage has not come up. What specifically is missing?"

"My aunt had some rather unusual French china, with a pink and gold border. Also items of silver: a large tray and a sixteenth-century tankard, along with some smaller serving pieces. I was wondering if by any chance she had packed them up for storage in the locker."

"I can't tell you at the moment, because, as I said, I haven't been down there since I moved in. To tell you the truth I find the place a bit scary. But I'll go down for a look and let you know."

"I really would appreciate it, Mrs. Bingham. The things in question have been in the family for years, and I can't imagine she would have sold them. She was my godmother and always said I was to have them. But she was an old lady, and who knows? I hate to put you out, but you are the only one who now has access to the locker. Please call me collect."

"A call to Toronto won't put me into the poorhouse. I'll go downstairs now and have a look. Will you be at home for the rest of the day?"

"Without doubt. I'm still recuperating, so I'm housebound."

As I replaced the receiver I realized that had I been my mother I would have inquired as to why she had been in the hospital, murmured sympathetically over the symptoms, and asked solicitously about her recuperation. But the wicked truth staring me in the face was that I did not really care.

I changed into jeans, picked up a ring of keys, and rode the elevator to the basement. I am not afraid of the dark, but I confess to a slight unease about being underground, especially in dimly lit spaces. Perhaps there were no real cobwebs, but there ought to have been. I would have been happier armed. Using my Yale key I opened the steel-plated fire door leading into the lockers. A single light switch turned on a few bare bulbs whose pale glow did not bolster confidence. I made my way to locker number 17, secured by a large padlock I had inherited from the previous owner.

The door of rough slats swung open to reveal a cavernous space half filled with miscellaneous items: two tires with heavy winter treads, rubber mats for the floor of a car, and a half empty jug of washer fluid. Pushed into a corner stood two rolls of broadloom beside an upright vacuum cleaner whose prototype must be stored in the Smithsonian Institute. Stacked beside a row of red clay pots, which once held house plants, were four cartons, two holding Christmas tree ornaments and the remaining two filled with books. Of the missing items described by Beatrice Lane I found no trace.

Retracing my steps, not without relief, I returned to my apartment and telephoned Mrs. Lane. She answered promptly, and I described the contents of the locker.

"Well, well," she concluded, "I guess my aunt must have sold the things. It seems odd, as she had always been quite definite about wanting them to come to me. But older people often worry about not having enough money, so who knows. In any case, I want to thank you for your trouble."

"Do you want the books?"

"No thanks, I'm swamped with books of my own, and they cost the earth to ship."

"Well, I guess that's it. Sorry I couldn't solve the mystery."

After a few more inconsequential remarks we rang off. No sooner had I replaced the receiver than I began to wonder about those two cartons of books. I too had been swamped with books in Victoria, both mine and Walter's. Sorting and discarding them had been the most onerous task of my move. I wanted to take them all, but the cost of shipping plus the logistics of finding space for them in an apartment convinced me I had to be stern. In the end I brought only three cartons: reference books, my favourite cookbooks, and a handful of volumes with strong sentimental value.

My intention was to buy bookcases or have a carpenter install shelves, possibly in the spare bedroom. Meanwhile, I wanted something to read and wondered if those two cartons might hold anything of interest. And since I was wearing jeans, and seeing as how I had just survived a visit to my locker and emerged unscathed, I decided to go back down to check out the books.

As I had suspected, most of the volumes turned out to be yellowing paperbacks: *The Scarlet Pimpernel*, *Turning Wheels*, *God's Little Acre*, several of the Fu Manchu series, and a clutch of Georgette Heyer Regency romances. The bottom layer of books consisted of cosy British murder novels: Christie, Marsh, Sayers. The second carton turned out to be more promising, as it held a number of the old Random House

Modern Library editions, most of which I had read long ago. Still, *Don Quixote*, *War and Peace*, *Bleak House* would look impressive on my shelves. A few slender volumes of poetry had been inscribed by the author. A quick glance told me that none of the poems rhymed, and I am too insensitive to read unstructured verse. One nugget was *Out of Africa*, a book by Isak Dinesen I had not yet read: another find turned out to be a collection of short stories that had originally appeared in *The New Yorker*.

A volume with no visible title on the spine turned out to be a journal or diary, the title page identifying it as belonging to Phyllis Donaldson, the previous owner of the apartment. It seemed odd that something as personal as a journal would end up in a carton of books that had seen better days. Perhaps I would mail it to Beatrice Lane. I added the journal to the pile of Modern Library editions I took upstairs.

By now it was too late for an afternoon nap, but after my substantial lunch I felt disinclined to organize the linen closet, a close second to the one opened weekly by Fibber McGee on his radio show. Instead, I sat on the one comfortable armchair, borrowed from Diana, and reached for Phyllis Donaldson's journal. I suppose reading someone else's diary is only one step removed from reading her mail, but had it been really important it would not have been stowed away in the locker wedged between George Gissing and Wilkie Collins.

Printed in copperplate script on the title page were the

words: "This Journal is the Property of" followed by a heavy black line on which was written "(Mrs.) Phyllis Donaldson." Below the signature in parentheses had been written "Volume 25." Evidently Mrs. Donaldson had been a woman who kept diaries; the previous volumes must have been packed and removed with the rest of her possessions. It seemed odd that what appeared to be the last volume had gone missing, but then so had my portraits of Keats and Lorca.

The urge to record one's life in a diary has always puzzled me, unless of course you are one of that select group who knows where the bodies are buried. For the rest, I can think of only two reasons for keeping a journal. Either you are so unsure of yourself that you have to verify your existence by writing it down (I record; therefore, I am); or your ego is so vast that you honestly believe future generations will want to read about the trivia of your daily life. "Friday: lunch with Freddie. We ate grilled sole and talked about reincarnation." People remember the things that are important to them; the rest is window dressing. I distrust both kinds of journal keepers. The country mice tend to be the kind of meekly bullying bores one would cross the street to avoid. "I'd like to tell you a story, but I'm sure you wouldn't be interested ..." The front-and-centre journal keepers are even worse. They blandly assume their innermost thoughts are of interest to mankind; furthermore, they record their dreams, an offense which ought to be written into the criminal code.

A glance at the opening paragraphs convinced me that Phyllis Donaldson wrote from a small rather than immense ego.

January 17: Just back from burying Arthur. Bitterly cold at the cemetery. I wished I had worn my down filled coat instead of the mink, but I had to sit in the front pew. I longed for something to cover my ears, not to mention woollen knickers. How they manage to dig a grave in that frozen earth I'll never know. Barbara, bless her heart, had the mourners back to her flat for tea, coffee, sherry, or punch. Party sandwiches, celery stuffed with cream cheese, tiny quiche and pizzas, petits fours, and an ice cream cake. I was glad to get home. Not that much has changed. When Arthur last went into the hospital I knew I was saying goodbye. The nice young man from across the hall came to the funeral and brought me home in a taxi. Very kind. I think I will give Arthur's clothing to a goodwill organization.

January 20: Lunch with Elsie, always tiresome as she insists on splitting the bill right down the middle. My meal cost five dollars more than hers, meaning I had to pay more tax and tip. I offered to pay for the whole thing, but she wouldn't hear of it. She carries a ziplock bag full of small change, so we worked it out down to the last 3 cents. She worries about my being alone. I pointed out that I have been on my own for the last six months, and the young man across the hall is keeping an eye on me.

Sometimes I wonder about the value of friends like Elsie. She means well, but all her fussing over the lunch cheque made us late for the movie. Would I have been better off eating alone and getting to the cinema on time? I think so, but being alone too much is bad for one, so they say.

January 31: Jonathan Barclay, the young man across the hall, invited me over to his flat for sherry. What a remarkable place. So full of beautiful things. He says he is a collector, and from time to time he sells things on commission. He has a tale to tell about every piece in his apartment. I have to confess I find him very amusing, and handsome. Odd that he has never married, but perhaps if he had a wife he wouldn't be so attentive to me.

February 6: I screwed up my courage and invited Jonathan for tea. I have not baked for some time now, so I made peanut butter cookies, scones, and a pound cake. I could have saved myself the trouble as he hardly ate a thing. Still, he is very droll. He appeared to be very interested in a number of things in my apartment, mostly silver and china. He also is very knowledgeable, telling me about hallmarks and china factories. Most men can't tell china from Tupperware. I feel very fortunate to have him as a neighbour.

The doorbell interrupted my reading. I took off my glasses and opened the door to find Jonathan in the hall, his teeth on display.

"I hope you're free for a drink, say around six? An old friend has just loomed up, and the prospect of an entire evening alone with him is just too dreary. Please come and put your shoulder to the wheel."

I hesitated. My dance card was empty; however, I did not wish to become the resident warm body, to be summoned when necessary. But as the old saw has it: "He who hesitates is lost." My silence translated itself into acquiescence.

"Don't bother to dress up," he announced airily, and was gone.

So much for my jeans. I had been ordered to change, but a small, rebellious voice whispered the unilateral directive, the one beginning with "F." Instead I went into the bathroom and under the harsh, uncompromising, fluorescent light, which I intended to replace, I did a number on my face. I began with eyeliner, then warm eye shadow on the lids to accentuate cobalt blue eyes (my principal vanity), a little blush to highlight good cheekbones which, along with an aquiline nose, help to anchor my face, or so I was assured during a cosmetic makeover Walter once gave me for my birthday. I took extra care with my lipstick, red but muted enough so that I don't look as though I will go for the throat. My pewter hair is cut short to take advantage of its natural wave. I wash it in the shower every morning, towel it dry, comb it, then forget it. The increments of crepe at the throat I looked on as war wounds, along with stretch marks and tits that no longer looked my reflection straight in the eye, souvenirs of a life lived.

Over my T-shirt and gold chain I wore one of Walter's oxford cloth, button down shirts, three of which I had found, never worn, in his dresser. I folded back the sleeves, the better to display several gold bangles, loot from a Caribbean cruise, and slid on a large aquamarine ring from Mexico. At the last minute I changed my Adidas for velvet slippers. Were I to be cast as the resident fag hag or fruit fly I would have to make the most of a limited wardrobe.

What the hell! At least Jonathan kept good scotch.

The man who opened the door when I rang the bell ought to have been photographed in a dinner jacket, leaning against the rail of an upscale cruise ship. Tall, greying, tanned, he looked as though he had been sprayed with Teflon or some other protective coating so that nothing even remotely offensive might cling.

"Good evening. You must be Louise. I'm Roger Clarke." A strong hand enveloped mine and drew me through the door. "Johnny's changing, and I have strict orders to give you a scotch and water without delay."

"Sounds good. Only please don't tell the Women's Christian Temperance Union."

He laughed easily, the kind of laughter that says in effect I am not here to burn down your house and kidnap the children. While he went into the kitchen to pour, leaving me momentarily alone, I looked around the large living room. The pink and gold china still held pride of place on the sideboard, but I noticed a handsome Georgian tankard sitting on a marble-topped commode with elaborate gilt handles on convex drawers, a type of furniture I particularly dislike. Could they possibly be the pieces once belonging to Phyllis Donaldson?

Further speculation was interrupted by the entrance of Jonathan in a nimbus of expensive male cologne and dressed with the studied casualness — loafers worn without socks, sweater with sleeves pushed up to the elbows — that takes no little time to achieve. He greeted me effusively, as though I had just returned from a long journey.

As I nursed my scotch, while the men drank martinis on the rocks, I came to realize that I had been invited not to help Jonathan entertain a trying guest, but to act as audience for their conversational sallies and arch dialogue. There was between them the easy intimacy which comes from long acquaintance. They may well have been lovers, pure speculation on my part, but why not go for the more interesting spin. In any event they needed me to behold them, to behave like the chorus in Greek drama, at once observing and commenting on the action.

"What brings you to Montreal?" I asked Roger. It was the basic "What do you do?" question slightly camouflaged.

"He has come to torment me," replied Jonathan. "Mind

you, it could be worse. At least he didn't bring his accordion."

"You are a bitch," drawled Roger, whose every gesture seemed geared to obtain maximum effect with minimum effort. "I've never played the accordion in my life. You have to have bad breath to play the accordion. What I've always longed to do is play jazz on the cello."

"I adore jazz played on stringed instruments," said Jonathan. "It brings a tear to my glass eye."

"Not to mention a blush to the freshly shaven cheek," I volunteered. "Heard any good concertos — concerti lately?"

Roger laughed out loud, while Jonathan bared his teeth. "Why are you here?" I inquired again. "And from whence?"

"He's from Ottawa," replied Jonathan. "He's an unscrupulous dealer, here to rip off my best pieces, at least that's his story for the press. What he really comes to Montreal for is sex and drugs and rock and roll."

"Sadly true," added Roger. "Ottawa is tranquil. If it weren't for pickpockets I wouldn't have any sex life at all."

I laughed out loud; and it occurred to me the men had been drinking before I arrived.

Jonathan exposed his teeth in what could have passed for a smile. "You've heard of heterosexual, Louise. And bisexual? Roger is tri-sexual. He'll try anything once."

"Jealousy, dear boy," said the unruffled Roger. "Your problem is that you couldn't get laid if you were a table at the Ritz."

"Don't talk while I am interrupting. It pisses me off."

Roger smiled. "Better to be pissed off than on."

I sat quietly, at once amused and a little taken aback. Was I watching *Private Lives* or *The Boys in the Band*? I am way past the age of being shocked, but this kind of borderline trash talk presupposed a familiarity I did not feel we had achieved.

Roger brandished his empty glass. "Is it my imagination, or has this gin been cut?"

"It has not been cut," replied Jonathan, lounging in the persimmon *bergère*, "but how long has it been since a mere forty per cent alcohol by volume could even get your blood circulating? You know your way to the bar. Top me up while you're at it."

While Roger was out of the room I seized my opportunity. "That's a handsome tankard. Did you have it last time I was here?"

"No, it was out being repaired." He rolled his eyes. "The previous owner used it to store pennies. The hinge on the lid was broken. She also owned the china with the pink border. Can you believe? She was using the sugar bowl to hold an African violet — and she used to put the plates into the dishwasher. Ah, here comes the martini elf."

Roger lowered himself onto a loveseat and for a while paid me the compliment of pretending to be interested. He asked how long I had been living at Queen's Court and why I had returned to Montreal. In five minutes he had learned more about me than Jonathan had since we met.

Unmarried people of a certain age, by that I mean men

and women over fifty, tend to become self-absorbed. Now that I am a widow I must be on guard, although I realized long ago that I learn nothing by talking about myself. Walter and I knew a number of single people in Victoria, divorced, widowed, gay. In their company I found myself being talked at, not to. Roger, however, had the knack of seeming to give me his full attention. Whether or not he really followed what I said, I found the illusion flattering. Jonathan appeared to listen, but his eyes focused on everything and nothing.

Although I had been invited for a drink, I confess I entertained the notion I might be asked to join the men for dinner. I liked Roger, and believed that, given half a chance, he would turn out to be interesting. On the other hand I was still reluctant to get too cosy with Jonathan, with whom I had to coexist on the fifth floor.

As it turned out, I did not have to decide. Jonathan looked at his watch, thin, rectangular, gold, and announced that they had better think of moving on, as friends were meeting them at the restaurant. In no uncertain terms I had been informed my time was up. Having provided an audience for the drinking hour, I had now outlived my usefulness. The sheer rudeness was almost comical; but like the elephant, I never forget.

I finished my drink and stood.

"So glad you could drop by," said Jonathan as he stood aside so I could walk to the door.

Roger followed me, possibly in an attempt to ease my abrupt departure. "It was a pleasure meeting you, Louise. If you find yourself in Ottawa give me a call. I'm in the directory: Roger Clarke, Antiques. Come by and see the shop. Then we could have lunch."

"I'd like that." We shook hands. I nodded goodnight to Jonathan, who replied with a bow.

And that was that.

꙳

One of Walter's favourite sayings was "You can't fly on one wing," meaning one drink is not enough. Granted, the scotch Roger poured for me had been a belt, but — as they say in the newspapers — closure demanded another pop. I poured myself a second, far weaker drink, added a generous dash of water, and settled down in the comfortable chair. Beside it on the floor lay the diary I had been reading when Jonathan rang the bell. I continued to read.

February 10: I ran into Jonathan in the elevator this morning, and he paid me the loveliest compliment. He said he was glad I wore nothing more than a little lipstick because I had such lovely skin I didn't need cosmetics. We chatted a bit in the hall. He told me that if I ever wanted to sell my china or silver he could probably find me a buyer. I'm not really interested in selling any of my things, but it's reassuring to know I could if I wanted to.

February 14: Jonathan invited me over for sherry. He doesn't drink sherry but keeps it for his friends. He told me he knows of someone who is looking for a Georgian tankard, just like mine. He could get me a very good price, and his commission is only 10%. I told him the tankard came from my late husband's family, and he would have wanted it to go to one of his nieces or nephews. I know it has value because when Arthur had it evaluated some years ago for insurance purposes it was said to be worth $8,000.00. I did say to Jonathan that if I ever changed my mind I would deal with no one but him. Then I foolishly asked him if he had a valentine. He half smiled and said he did, but she doesn't know it yet.

February 20: Jonathan came for dinner. I bought a nice sirloin steak, but he only ate a few bites along with some salad. He brought his own martinis in a jug, as I have never had much of a head for gin. It was pleasant to cook dinner for a man again. Arthur was ill for so long that I made most of his meals in a blender. After dinner Jonathan asked if he could see the rest of my silver, the pieces I hadn't used for dinner. Most of them came from Arthur's family and are quite old. Jonathan particularly liked my Sheffield tray, way too large for me, but what can one do.

The telephone interrupted my reading; I recognized my son's number and the 604 Vancouver area code.

"Craig! What's up?"

"Hi, Louise. How's it going. Are you settling in?"

"More or less. Every day in every way. Is this strictly a social call?"

"Not completely. I find I have to come to Montreal for a few days — I'm not yet sure just how long — and I was wondering if I could use your spare room. You did say you had an extra bedroom, or am I having an early senior moment?"

"No, I do have a so-called guest room, only I haven't gotten around to furnishing it yet. I didn't expect you to come east so soon. When are you arriving?"

"Day after tomorrow. Not to worry. I'll find a room in one of those small tourist hotels down by the bus station."

"That would break your old, grey-haired, mother's heart. I have a better idea. Why don't you move into the apartment; it's spare but liveable, and I'll stay with Diana."

"I hate to push you out of your new apartment. You've only just moved in."

"Not at all. Why spend money on a hotel? I'd rather you took me out to dinner."

"Well — if you're sure it's okay."

"Let me know when you will be arriving. I have voice mail. I'll be here to let you in and give you the key."

"You're sure Aunt Diana won't mind?" The "aunt" was a courtesy title. Both Walter and I had discouraged our children from using first names with adults.

"Believe it or not, she was sorry to see me leave. And you know Diana. Money spent on hotels, taxis, or drinks in a bar is money down the drain. I'll see you soon."

I telephoned Diana. As anticipated, she offered her spare room to either me or Craig, but I knew she would be more comfortable with me underfoot than my son. And the prospect of seeing Craig more than outweighed the modest inconvenience of having to relocate.

4

raig is my son from my first marriage, a love child if ever there was one. I met his father, an unbelievably gorgeous Slav, during that brief period in late adolescence when hormones combine with imagination to translate sexual desire into romantic longing. His Christian name did not end with a consonant, and he came from a postal code no one in my family even knew existed. But I didn't care. I would have followed him to Siberia, which I subsequently came to realize is not unlike Canada, only without Toronto.

Before meeting Serge I had weathered my share of crushes. One — a not-bad-looking boy with a crew cut and horn-rimmed glasses — I even considered marrying. Upon leaving university he shed his left-wing views, went to law school, and moved somewhere to the right of Louis XIV. At the time

I was working as a secretary, and he needed a wife who held a university degree or who, at the very least, had been a deb. He respected me, which is another way of saying he did not try to remove my knickers; and after two unsuccessful marriages he finally exploded from the closet and began to lobby for same-sex unions.

I was still a virgin when I met Serge, but on our first date my legs rose into the air as if attached to pulleys. I turned out to be a quick study, and in no time flat had earned an "A" in screwing. To my astonishment Serge fell in love with me, largely I think because I did not have thick red arms and hands that could drain a cow's udder in minutes. I also told him on occasion that he was full of shit, although I phrased it more delicately. As it turned out, I was as exotic to him as he to me. One night, after a fuck during which the earth might not have moved but I certainly did, he asked me to marry him. I think I said yes before he had finished popping the question.

My own mother, a soap opera queen, dithered, and wrung her hands, and wept over the prospect of losing her only daughter, and enjoyed herself so much I could have shaken her. Father grunted and shrugged, secretly delighted another man was prepared to shoulder the financial burden. Serge was an orphan, which to someone raised on Dickens only added to his romantic appeal. Such relatives as there were did not speak much English, so I never did figure out where they stood on the wedding.

The real disapproval, none the less forceful for being unspoken, came from Diana's parents, my Aunt Charlotte and Uncle Ian. They already had my father, a case study in downward mobility, to contend with; and now their niece and surrogate sister to their daughter Diana had announced she intended to marry someone from abroad. I would have preferred their approval; they had been good to me during my youth and adolescence, but their silent censure rested on a system of values a century out of date. Nothing fans the fires of romantic passion more than barriers, be they geographical, financial, or social. I almost longed for more insurmountable obstacles so that my champion might enter the lists, my sleeve fluttering from his helmet, perhaps not to kill the opposition but to knock it smack on its ass.

Instead of indulging me in drama, opposition, ultimata, Aunt Charlotte and Uncle Ian chose to accept the inevitable, don beige lace and morning coat, and smile blandly while a Unitarian minister pronounced us man and wife. Diana stood by as matron of honour.

On our wedding night we stopped taking precautions. With no family of his own, Serge wanted children even more than I. As far as I was concerned, motherhood could wait for a while, at least until the novelty of not having to go to work every morning had worn off. But the best-laid plans and so forth. I am pretty sure Craig was conceived on our wedding night. Whatever misgivings I may have entertained went down before Serge's boundless enthusiasm. To my open-mouthed astonishment he expressed the hope that our first child would be a girl so that she could give me a hand raising the younger children and leave me free to have a life outside the hearth and home. There would be sons; Serge wanted children whenever they came. Why else did he work hard to build up a business?

I did not have answers; happiness blunts the mind. For the one and only time in my life I looked into the mirror and thought myself beautiful. And why not? My entire metabolism had gone into overdrive. I floated in a gondola down a Venetian canal with no immediate destination. I did not even wish for one, so immersed was I in the present moment.

The journey ended late one night while driving home from a boisterous party in the Laurentians. Serge was at the wheel, and he must have nodded off for a moment, as suddenly we pitched into a ditch. The couple in the back seat were more startled than shaken up. I bruised my legs, and Serge died. A sharp blow on the head was the verdict of the coroner. Who knows or cares. In a flash I stopped living in blazing technicolour and moved into black and white.

Some experiences are difficult to remember: extreme pain, great happiness, intense grief; but I managed to salvage two things from my brief marriage. The first was my son Craig, the second a memory of a bond almost literary in its intensity. An ordinary woman had known an extraordinary love with an ordinary man. Serge had died before our marriage grew stale or routine. And for that reason I have never ceased to love him, even now. That in itself is an austere, Canadian kind of comfort, but I know no other kind.

Nature is said to abhor a vacuum in much the same way that I abhor a vacuum cleaner. The grieving widow found herself upstaged by the role of new mother, at best an over-whelming bit of casting. I was fortunate in having a doting mother, besotted with her first grandson and eager to mind him anytime, anyplace. When the dust had finally settled, the modest amount of life insurance Serge had left went to pay debts and funeral expenses. My former boss had gone through three secretaries since my departure and welcomed me back. Nowadays single working mothers are thick on the ground, but forty years ago such was not the case.

I had a series of what were then called affairs, today known as relationships. (Affairs were more fun.) Sean O'Connor, with whom I recently had lunch, headed up the list which, I suppose, is another way of saying I seriously considered marrying him. Craig had turned into a textbook child, bright, even tempered, and given to sleeping through the night. What parent could ask for more? When he was not under my care he was with Mother. Masculine influence was slight, but I was still unprepared to marry someone just so he would be a father for my son.

Then I met Walter Bingham, widowed, handsome, conservative, and I felt as though I had seen landfall after a bumpy voyage. He had a daughter, I a son. He wanted a wife, and I filled the job description. Another plus is that he made a wonderful stepfather for Craig.

Was I as good a mother? As the French say in the Province of Quebec, "I did my possible." From an early age Craig had been a focused child, absorbed in whatever task lay at hand. I tried to interfere as little as I could, only pulling rank when I honestly believed it necessary. I talked to him about the birds and the bees; Walter told him about sex. I lobbied for table manners, root vegetables, standard usage, clean socks, and homework. Never did I have the slightest interest in sports and games; neither did Walter. Consequently when Craig, who had inherited his father's lean, muscular physique, evinced no interest in hockey, football, baseball, basketball, track, or the rest of those sweaty endeavours endorsed by what used to be called He-men, his parents did not think him odd. We all listened to the Met broadcasts on Saturday afternoons, went to the ballet, and bought him his own record player.

More important, as it turned out, we took him to art galleries, initially at our instigation, then at his. At an early age he grew bored with colouring books, the kind with heavy black lines defining the areas to be filled in with crayon, and took to drawing freehand. There was no looking back. He is now an artist; furthermore, he pays the rent with his painting.

ᔐ

"SON AND HEIR!"

"Venerable mother!"

"You're a sight for these rheumy old eyes," We embraced.

Craig put his bag against the wall and looked around. "Say, Louise, this is pretty nice. The rooms are so well laid-out you don't really need furniture."

"That's reassuring. I do plan to acquire some, but the days slip away. I don't have a car, and most of the warehouse stores are on the outskirts of town. How long do you intend to stay?"

"Not long. I don't want to evict you from your own home. Besides, I have to go to New York. Unfortunately world events have not been favourable for the art market, but New York is still the place to be."

"Have you thought about moving back east?"

Craig laughed. "Not more than three or four times a day. But so many of those slightly derelict commercial buildings that were ideal for studios have been turned into upscale condos. Yesterday's squat is today's prestige address."

"You might consider moving to one of the smaller cities within easy commuting distance of Montreal, like Cowansville or Drummondville. Would you like some coffee?"

"Not at the moment, thanks. It will stunt my growth." The last was one of our private jokes, as Craig stood a good six feet. He took after his father, tall, lean, handsome, only he had my blue eyes which, with his curly black hair made an arresting combination.

"I have the makings of breakfast. Have you eaten?"

"No, but I have a better idea. Let me take you out for breakfast. We can catch up over eggs Benedict."

We walked a few short blocks to a restaurant that specialized in egg dishes. The sign over the door read "EGGSactly (as you want them)". Craig made a wry face, and we went inside. Fortunately we were a bit late for the regular breakfast crowd, as the restaurant was one vast reflective surface with nothing to absorb noise. We chose a booth near a window. Without consulting the menu we ordered eggs Benedict and coffee, then turned to catching up.

Craig had come to Victoria shortly before I flew east, so I filled him in on the pitfalls of house hunting, settling in, unpacking, and generally readjusting. I did not tarry over details and concluded my tale with the observation that so far things had been going pretty well. Walter used to say that when everything is coming your way you're in the wrong lane, but such was my pleasure in seeing Craig that I couldn't help putting a positive spin on my decision to come east.

Craig got equal time. He told of how he believed it was time for him to move east, at least for part of the year. He preferred life on the West Coast and still hoped to spend the winter months far from snow and ice. But he now felt ready to undertake the Toronto/Montreal/New York art scene. He already had galleries in Vancouver, Seattle, and San Francisco; but Craig was ambitious. I understood he wanted more money, as who does not; but more than just the money he wanted the career. He believed in the tradition of figurative painting, of still life and landscape. He had painted a few portraits even though most people prefer to face a camera. He mistrusted trends, fads, fashions. Installation art brought out the rhetoric of denunciation. Not only did he believe in the figurative tradition, he wanted to matter, to make a contribution that would last. Craig had intimations of immortality backed up by talent and determination. I could only hope he would realize one day he had reached his destination and not spend his life watching this destination recede into the vanishing distance of impossible expectations.

Craig paid the bill and we left the background noise of the restaurant for the less intense noise of the street. As Craig kissed me on both cheeks, I spoke. "I'll walk back to the apartment and collect my bag. As you well know, there are no free favours. Diana expects you for dinner this evening, after which you will be off the hook. If we could have lunch one day, *tant mieux*. I've alerted the management that you will be staying in the apartment, so there shouldn't be any problem. See you around six."

Back at Queen's Court I packed an overnight case, carried it out to the elevator, and pushed the "Down" button. An aureole of red surrounding the button indicated the elevator to be on its way.

A woman, no longer young, came to stand beside me; I recognized her as one of the residents of my floor. I half smiled and gave a small nod of recognition. She nodded without smiling before giving the button a sharp jab, even though the elderly appliance was giving off a reassuring series of rattles and clanks suggesting its imminent arrival. I was tempted to observe that I had received a passing grade at Elevator-Button-Pushing School but reconsidered. The way she whacked the button suggested an absence of humour.

The door jerked open, and I followed her into the thick air of the box, heavy with the residue of expensive perfumes. Most of the women living in Queen's Court were collecting the old-age pension. As such they had been young women at a time when perfume was as much a part of their *toilette* as lipstick. The habit continued long past the age to entice. Still they slathered on the scent, leaving their overlapping spoor in the elevator like a miasma of perfume cards. Or, as Walter would have said, "The miasma is bad for my asthma." He said things like that. But I always forgave him.

◞

February 27: I was waiting for the elevator when Jonathan joined me. He offered me a lift to the supermarket, so much nicer than the bus. He asked me if I knew what a treasure I had in my pink and gold china. If I stopped ruining it by putting it into the dishwasher he could sell it for a price that would help send me on a cruise. I have to confess I was tempted. It's not as though it came from my own family. And I would like to accommodate Jonathan. My life has been so much more agreeable since we struck up an acquaintance. Not to mention that the idea of a cruise is tempting. I wonder if Jonathan would want to come along. Of course he wouldn't want to spend that much time with an older woman. But it would be delightful if he did.

March 3: Edna called, wanting me to make a fourth at bridge, but I begged off, saying I was busy. Jonathan may call, and I would hate to be out if he did. He is very keen to have my cocktail shaker, even if it is only silver plate. He insists it is a fine example of art deco, and he knows someone who is a collector. I certainly never drink cocktails, and I don't know anyone who does. Perhaps I'll let him sell it. We could discuss the deal over tea or sherry, perhaps a drink. I bought a bottle of gin and a small one of vermouth. Carrying a jug of martinis through the hall strikes me as common. And Jonathan is certainly not that. I think he is perhaps the most interesting man I have ever met.

March 4: Jonathan did not call. But I am not sorry I missed bridge with Edna. She is a timid player and doesn't really understand how to bid. I expect he will call today. After all, I am not going to insist he take the cocktail shaker. A little coaxing never hurt. The days are really getting longer. Spring is definitely on the way.

I put the diary onto the night table, considered reaching for my novel, then turned off the light. Phyllis Donaldson was not about to win any posthumous awards for her prose, but I found the diary interesting because of location. I also knew one of the players. It looked to me as though P.D. was developing a huge crush on J.B., more fool she.

During those brief moments before impending sleep blurred consciousness, I thought about Craig. Dinner had been pleasant; Diana telephoned one of her caterers, so all we had to do was reheat. Craig paid her court, then excused himself to see the last showing of a movie. He was welcome. Between the whispering patrons, cellphones, sticky floors, deafening advertisements, and pervasive odour of stale coconut oil, going to the movies has turned into an obstacle course.

Craig is forty-two, handsome, and unmarried. By today's frankly permissive standards that is not an indictment. Moreover, he has always been a loner, even as a child. I never felt compelled to propel him into sociability; neither did Walter. Craig had a few, select, close friends, but he was never what used to be called a party animal. I respected his privacy. As the youngest child in a household of men I hated the promiscuous togetherness that family life imposed. My own escape lay through my cousin Diana, only child of affluent parents. We bonded through being the same age and sex; her large, dim, tranquil house became my refuge from raised voices, mountains of dirty underpants, and crude practical jokes. Consequently, when Craig began early to express a preference for solitude, quiet, privacy, it struck me as the most natural thing in the world, in spite of what overly attentive elementary school teachers tried to persuade me to the contrary.

As he matured, young women found him irresistible, or so it seemed to me. Swooning school and college girls clustered around his tall good looks and air of diffidence like moths to a flame, to coin a phrase. Whether by inclination or strategy, Craig seemed indifferent to all this easy adulation. Distance lends enchantment; the more remote he acted, the more he found himself under siege. I never learned whether he quietly and efficiently made out, or whether his apparent lack of interest meant just that. I was not so naïve as to ignore the alternative explanation, but even if he were gay he did not drape himself in rainbow colours. There were a few male friends, none of whom could be described as jocks. Nor were they, to borrow an expression of my own mother, "light on their feet." And nobody ever got to heaven tossing a football into the neighbour's garden or blocking traffic to play hockey with a tennis ball.

At the risk of appearing to be an irresponsible parent, I didn't much care one way or the other. Ignorance may not necessarily be bliss, but too much wisdom imposes its own limitations. I did not long for grandchildren. Walter's daughter from his first marriage married rebelliously and young, bore three children as quickly as was humanly possible, then divorced. Walter shouldered the financial burden of his grandchildren and saw them staunchly through to majority.

I approved, although his responsibility demanded sacrifice on our part. Many were the trips not taken, the new cars postponed, the clothes bought on sale, all so college fees could be paid.

Unfortunately, when the smoke cleared away I realized I did not much like my step-grandchildren. I find them almost pathologically self-absorbed, attentive only when they want something, usually at once. One of the many pluses of moving to Montreal is leaving them on the West Coast. If they wish to see me, a likelihood I seriously doubt, they know where to find me. Nor do I much care whether Craig has children. At one point, when my life was more settled and the future stretched ahead in an unbroken line, I might have welcomed more grandchildren. But Serge died a long time ago, and now Walter is dead. Perhaps I should long for the continuity of new life, as Real Women might argue, but now? Another grandchild might be a welcome event, but I did not intend to lose sleep.

I did not. At three A.M. I awoke because I had to pee, then suddenly it was seven o'clock. How could the morning have arrived so quickly?

It had, with Diana under full sail. I knew she was pleased to have me once again under her roof; the cooked breakfast, which I did not want, afforded ample proof. But since it lurked in the DNA to disapprove, she had already made it clear that, as far as she was concerned, one should never lend anything, anything at all, to anyone to whom one has given birth. Even as I sipped my coffee and glanced at the paper I knew Diana believed that Craig was easing a woman (perhaps not a tart, but no better than she should be) out of my apartment at Queen's Court, and to hell with the doorman.

I also knew such was not the case, as Craig would never behave in such a manner as to compromise me or my apartment. What I also realized, and Diana did not, was that she cut her own children so little slack that they plotted and schemed to get away with whatever they could. Perhaps I am not being fair to her oldest son, a man who always thinks twice before saying nothing and who does not have a devious bone in his body. He is also the most boring man I know, but in fairness to Diana I have to say he takes after his father.

Diana does not suffer from stress; she's a carrier. No sooner had I removed the reading glasses, only recently acquired as an alternative to having my arms surgically stretched, than she pounced.

"Louise, I can't remember whether or not I told you, but I am in charge of the Christmas bazaar this year at St. Luke-the-Apostle. I was hoping you might be able to give me a hand. I need a volunteer to take care of Knitting and Needle-point, and another to look after Attic Treasures."

"I'm not your man — sorry, person. I lack the requisite sensitivity for either of those jobs. And you must remember your garage sale. I volunteered to help, and we ended up not speaking for almost a year."

Diana paused to regroup. "That was different. And we both agreed that particular sale is ancient history. But in this instance you will be working with masses of volunteers. You can make all sorts of new friends. And it is for the church, after all."

"Diana, climb down off your moral high horse. When I think about the murder, mayhem, torture, repression, and God only knows what all else inflicted on the world by the Christian Church, I do not wish to aid and abet it by flogging hand-knitted baby clothes. Besides, I'm a Unitarian and St. Luke is Church of England. It wouldn't do at all."

"Louise, do try to be sensible for a moment. We are not using the money to finance another Crusade or underwrite the Inquisition. We do not burn Unitarians at the stake; we do not extract confessions by forcing them to listen to Anglican hymns. What we do need is a new furnace to help safeguard the building — which I might add has been designated as a heritage site."

"Let me think it over. I'll have my people get back to your people." I carried my dishes over to the dishwasher. If selling other people's discards at the St. Luke bazaar was my trade-off for staying with Diana, I'd book a suite at the Old Brewery Mission.

"By the way," added Diana as she patted the newspaper together for recycling, "there is a phone message for you, from Sean O'Connor. He wants you to call. I meant to tell you yesterday, but seeing Craig put it quite out of my mind.

His name and number are on my desk."

I lost no time in returning the call, fortunately catching Sean before he went out. He invited me to have dinner with him this evening, and I accepted. Only after I had hung up did I realize I would be leaving Diana stranded. She had spoken of a possible late afternoon movie followed by something to eat. But, selfishly, I wanted to have dinner with Sean much more than to go to a movie with Diana.

On my way back to the kitchen I decided to cut a deal. In exchange for begging off tonight I would agree to work for her Christmas bazaar — in Attic Treasures. I lacked the inner fire to hustle Knitting and Needlepoint.

As it turned out, Diana had forgotten about a bridge date already penciled in for this evening. Had I but waited I would not have found myself committed to her Christmas bazaar, but that particular hurdle lay over two months away. My most pressing problem was what to wear this evening. Nothing I had brought with me to Diana's passed muster for dinner with an old beau, or sometime lover, to be less coy. What I needed was hanging in my apartment. I telephoned Craig to say I would be dropping by, but he did not answer. After my own voice informed me I was unable to come to the telephone at the moment, I left a message saying I was on my way over.

The doorman, tall, gaunt, morose, managed a faint smile as I entered the lobby. After collecting my mail I rode the elevator, reeking of Chanel No. 5. I buzzed twice and waited, giving Craig time to pull on some clothes if necessary. Somewhat gingerly I turned the key in the lock; my "Anybody home?" raised no reply. Going straight to my bedroom closet I lifted down my navy blue dress with matching coat to lay on the bed prior to choosing shoes.

It was then I realized the bed had not been used. As I had not yet bought a counterpane, I had covered the bed with a clean double sheet, tucking it neatly under the pillows to simulate a bolster. The striped sheet lay pristinely in place, unwrinkled, untouched, just as I had left it. Even were Craig to have made the bed before going out, I seriously doubt he would have bothered to replace the sheet-slash-bedspread exactly as found, satin-smooth and wrinkle-free. It would appear the bed had not been slept in, but that was not my concern. I have never been the kind of alarmist parent who called the police if she saw the police, so I did not jump to the conclusion that Craig lay bruised and bleeding in some emergency ward. Besides, dishes stacked neatly in the sink suggested he had made himself coffee this morning, along with a light breakfast. I folded my dress into a small suitcase, tossed in shoes and accessories, and left the apartment.

As a younger man Sean had been ultra conservative, certainly regarding clothes. He used to dress like an ageing preppie: button-down collars, striped or knitted ties, natural-shoulder jackets, chinos, penny loafers emblazoned with pennies found in the street. I never had to worry about dressing up to go out with him; what I wore to the office was more than suitable for a night on the town. My own taste is fairly conservative — no lamé, bugle beads, or marabou in my closet; but I decided to play it safe, not quite gloves and dyed-to-match-shoes safe, but suitable for a memorial service or annual meeting. I tarted up the basic-little-nothing navy blue dress with plenty of gold jewellery and more makeup than usual.

Since I had a few minutes to put in before calling a cab — I was to meet Sean at the restaurant — I stayed in my room and read a bit more of Phyllis Donaldson's small, precise calligraphy.

March 10: Jonathan rang my bell quite unexpectedly to hand me a pot of hyacinths. They have just come into bloom and are so wonderfully fragrant. I can smell them everywhere in the apartment. I was so delighted that I let him have the cocktail shaker for his client. When will I ever use it. I tried to pin him down for some supper, perhaps a little sole, rice, salad; but he is always on the go. Such an interesting life. I mentioned the title of a movie I wanted to see, and he suggested we might go together to an afternoon showing, and then perhaps have tea at the Ritz. I said that if he paid for the movie I'd shout him to tea. I hope we can do it soon.

March 12: An unusual occurrence this morning. After doing a bit of shopping I came into the building to find Jonathan having an altercation with the doorman. They did not raise their voices, but spoke with the kind of intensity that suggests anger barely held in check. I confess I was surprised. Both men have been so kind to me I find it distressing that they should so obviously be cross with one another. Of course the doorman couldn't say too much for fear of losing his job, but I could read rage in his posture. It's a shame we all can't get along better. The world would be a much better place if we could.

March 15: Jonathan told me that this week is frightfully busy for him. He has some kind of antique fair he must attend. So we will go to our movie and have tea sometime next week. Something to look forward to. It will almost be like going out on a date.

A glance at my watch reminded me that I too had a date, and perhaps I had better go downstairs and have Diana's doorman call me a cab. I have always believed that the mere fact of being a woman does not permit one to be late. A wag once observed that solitude is the reward for being punctual. Maybe so, but punctuality gives leverage. I was putting my best foot forward, a foot almost teetering on heels I rarely wear. But they do good things for my legs. I just have to remember to be careful on stairs.

༄

Not surprisingly, I was the first to arrive and was shown to a table by a woman who had obviously taken great pains to coax her hair into a semblance of post-coital disarray. I would have thought the look more suitable for a nightclub than a bistro, but this was Montreal. I wasn't in Kansas any-more. The restaurant itself trumpeted the dictum that less is more: bare floors, bentwood chairs, white tablecloths. All too often less is merely less, but Sean had vouched for the food.

I ordered a scotch and water, and glanced at the menu, so pan-continental the prices ought to have been printed in Euros. I watched a man, bald, overweight, perspiring, lean across a table towards his date, a young woman who sat stiff and upright, as if wearing a foundation garment that did not fit. The scene suggested a seduction that was not unfolding as it should; but if she really felt the way her posture suggested, then why had she gone to dinner with the man in the first place? My own mother, who never met an old saw she didn't like, used to say, "An ounce of prevention is worth a pound of cure." It is a good recipe for dating. If you don't like the guy, don't go out with him; there are worse things than staying home on a Saturday night.

Sean arrived looking more preppoid than preppy. In the bad old days he wore a tie when we ate out; tonight he wore a crew-necked sweater and jogging shoes. I felt relieved to have dressed down rather than up, although I could just as easily have worn my denim.

"I should have specified 'dress casual'," he said after we had exchanged the easy formulas of goodwill, "but you look terrific."

"Just grabbed the first thing out of the closet. There wasn't much choice. I discarded a lot of clothes before the move. No more twin sets and tweed. No more bandanas or Tilley Endurable hats. 'There'll be some changes made today!' (I sing through my nose by ear.) I plan to buy some new clothes, but first I have to buy furniture." I went on to explain how Craig was using my apartment, hence my sojourn with Diana.

"I wondered why you weren't at home. Craig told me you were at Diana's, but he didn't elaborate. I thought perhaps she was sick or something, but when I telephoned there was the good-old, five-thousand-volt Diana."

I laughed. "Diana is a genuine treasure, but like most treasures she demands high maintenance. The next time Craig comes for a visit I will have a bed for the spare room. Are you going to have a drink?"

"Of course. A double so I can catch up. Are you ready for another?"

"Why not. Do you know what you are going to eat?" (A wise woman once told me never to ask a man what he wants for dinner unless he is buying.)

"I always like the veal," he replied. "I'm not much of a fish feeder, and red meat these days comes with potatoes, salad, and medical baggage."

"Would you like me to order for you?" I asked, batting my lashes.

We shared a laugh at an old private joke. I have always believed that women who suggest their date order for them

97

deserve either the cheapest or least appealing item on the menu.

"How about the Veal *Zurichoise*? I've had it here and it passes muster."

"Sounds good."

"Will you have wine?"

"No thanks. I'll stick to my scotch, less headache-inducing even if evidence of a blunted palate."

"I'll place the order, then you can continue to fill me in."

Although we had done most of our catching up over the recent lunch, I expanded on my reasons for moving to Montreal. I did not dwell on Walter's death. What was to be gained by describing details about his terminal illness. Walter died, and that is all one needs to know.

I was also suitably brief. In spite of his *pro forma* interest in what I had been doing, I knew Sean was only marginally interested. His curiosity did not extend past the table of contents to the text; furthermore, so long as I was talking about myself he could not in all courtesy talk about himself. As a result, I unclipped my feminist epaulettes and settled in to drawing him out. After all, he was buying me dinner and, at the risk of sounding like a sellout, I was quite happy to sit back, eat, drink, and listen as he told of his travels.

I felt a little like the wedding guest stopped by the Ancient Mariner, compelled to listen; however, I was being bribed with an excellent dinner. At the same time I found myself both amused and bemused at the universal assumption that having travelled *ipso facto* makes a person more interesting.

To have survived a visit to Queen Hat-Shep-Sut's temple, to have promenaded along the Great Wall of China, to have roller skated past the treasures of the Hermitage, the Louvre, or the Vatican, somehow raises a person's stock on the Fascination Index. My problem with this socially accepted belief is that most valid experiences of travel are aesthetic; and no matter how deep and profound the impact of a building, a painting, a performance, or a geo-graphical wonder, these raptures do not translate easily into everyday conversation. "Magnificent, Breathtaking, Wonderful, Splendid, Awesome, To die for": the vocabulary of most aesthetic discourse is as limited as that for pornography or the supernatural.

To Sean's credit he had words at his disposal and was able to transcend the two-dimensional anecdotes of bedbugs and bad food. At times I could have envied his being there, in particular his visit to St. Petersburg, as he did not take a tour and could therefore spend real time at the Hermitage. I asked the right questions and became so engrossed in his description of Kyoto that I absentmindedly said yes to coffee, which ordinarily I never drink after noon.

When Sean invited me back to his apartment for a brandy I accepted without hesitation. Between the scotch, the coffee, and going out on a date for the first time in decades I was so wired there was no point in even considering sleep. Why not keep going?

I offered to pay for a cab. Sean lived in a formerly working-class neighbourhood now undergoing intense gentrification, as evidenced by front doors painted taupe, mushroom, shrimp, khaki, or avocado, and all illuminated by a matching pair of carriage lamps. Bamboo blinds and louvered shutters discouraged prying eyes. Window boxes and hanging planters supplemented handkerchief-sized lawns enclosed by meticulous fences. Sean lived on the third floor of a former townhouse now divided into three flats. The décor, spare, tasteful, reflected his travels: the bronze head of a Buddha, a framed papyrus of hieroglyphics, an angular Russian icon. Books on steel shelves lined the walls. The space was more than a pad, less than a house. I suspected Sean lived on a tight budget.

Over a brandy he told me how the owner of the building was terminating the three leases so he could restore the house for his married daughter. Family ties prevailed with the *Régie des Rentes*, and Sean had no choice but to move. I asked whether he intended to take all his books, remembering my recent cull in Victoria. He admitted he had already called a dealer who was coming next week. I told him about my own move and how I came to realize some books are just books, while others are valued objects and as such cannot be discarded.

Sean laughed and said as far as he was concerned all his books were objects. Then he put down his brandy snifter and kissed me. I was surprised, but not into immobility. I co-operated to the fullest extent. When had I last French-kissed, soul-kissed, or deep-kissed a man? (When I made love with Walter, kissing was not part of the routine, particularly as he liked sex first thing in the morning before we had brushed our teeth.) But with Sean I put my heart into the soul-kiss and, as E.H. might have said, "It was good."

My astonishment sprang from finding myself the object of Sean's affection. His last lady love could have passed for his daughter. Why me, when the city teemed with chicks and available women younger than I. Why indeed? But now was not the time for abstract speculation, as two more kisses later, (Three's a charm!) Sean suggested we repair to the bedroom.

He had the tact not to turn on the light. Late middle age is kinder to men than to women, and even though neither of us had put on weight, I could see in the dim light that Sean had been less affected by the tug of gravity than I. Uncomfortable though they may have been, garter belts and stockings were easier and sexier to remove than pantyhose. Moderately arthritic shoulders have persuaded me to buy bras that fasten in front, so that bit of disrobing I managed alone.

Naked, I lost no time in sliding under the covers to join Sean, who had fewer clothes to remove. Our bodies shared a memory that did not require narrative. Making love was more like a familiar tune played on an only slightly out-of-tune piano. Older men take their time, luckily for me as I was a bit out of practice. Television sitcoms aside, most women do not want more inches but minutes. Maybe the coloured lights were a bit more pastel, possibly the roller coaster seemed less precipitous, perhaps the waves heaved rather than crashed against the rocks; but we still managed a Canada Day spectacular. "And it was good."

Now for the pillow talk. Could I remember what arch things to say after so many years as a bourgeois housewife?

"At least I no longer have to worry about birth control," I volunteered. "My child-bearing days have joined the snows of yesteryear."

In the dark Sean chuckled. "Nothing like a bit of gynaecological François Villon under the circs. But we're doubly protected. I had a vasectomy."

"You what? Don't answer. I heard you the first time. Why?"

"The young lady I was seeing was afraid of the pill. And I dislike wearing condoms. So we compromised. At my age I took it as a compliment."

"Well, well." (Walter used to say that a vasectomy means never having to say you're sorry, but I decided to keep that one to myself.)

"I have to admit, Louise, you haven't lost the knack."

"Neither have you. And you have done wonders for my self-esteem. You know the old joke about older women being like the South Pole. Everybody knows where it is, but nobody goes there."

"Please don't talk of yourself as older. We are the same age — the same middle age."

"Point taken. And now, my dear Sean, I will arise and go. Before you make polite noises about my staying over, believe me, I would prefer to. But then I would have to face Diana. I'm too old to begin making up alibis about how we ran into old friends and ended up hanging out until the wee hours. Nor do I want to confront her with the truth. She will think I should still be in mourning, and I hate to give her the moral edge. Better that I leave."

Sean did not press me to stay. Why would he? Mornings after can be trying. We all have our routines for coming to grips with a new day, and former lovers do not fit easily into the scheme, at least not on the first reencounter. I would have enjoyed another morning fuck, but I did not want to cook breakfast in my good outfit. Sean would have expected no less. I left him once because he was a closet chauvinist, and nothing he had said or done this evening persuaded me otherwise.

By the time I returned to my temporary home, Diana had gone to bed. No light seeped under her bedroom door, but I made a little discreet noise in case she had not yet fallen asleep. I felt almost like a teenager putting one over on the chaperone. And yet, had Craig been using my spare room, would I have stayed out all night? I doubt it. Not that he would have minded, but I would just as soon keep my affairs to myself.

As I drifted off to sleep I realized, almost with relief, that I was no longer the least bit in love with Sean. In fact, I no longer want to be in love with anyone. Being in love puts you at the mercy of a stranger, and after all these years Sean was no longer the man I had once known. Being in love is for the young; its condition of temporary insanity requires great energy. At this point in my life I wanted a good uncomplicated fuck without *son et lumière*. Whether Sean would continue to provide that delicious commodity remained to be seen.

I awoke around four, uncomfortably aware of the tomato sauce I had eaten at dinner. Middle age means dropping antacid, but the calcium is supposed to be good for disintegrating bones. Every cloud has a lead lining.

5

*W*earing my nonchalance like a new outfit, I ventured out of my room, only to find a note beside the coffee machine informing me Diana had gone out. She did not specify where, nor did she leave any instructions about meals or shopping. I was not surprised. Diana has organized her life so as not to experience it, being constantly in motion her method of keeping solitude at bay. One of the annoying features of visiting Diana is that she doesn't subscribe to a newspaper. Walter and I received two morning papers to avoid conflict. Coffee with newsprint is my preferred way to begin the day. Such magazines as Diana was sent dealt with issues of health, finance, and the better brands of vcr, nothing I wanted to undertake with coffee. For want of anything better, I returned to the diary.

It turned out to be a discouraging choice. Turning the page I found one last, cryptic entry.

March 29: I will have to cancel my date with Jonathan. The cancer has come back, and the doctor insists I go into hospital immediately for treatment. How I hate to go. I fear the hospital more than the illness. I will give Jonathan my key and ask him to water my plants. This will probably be my last entry for a while. And just when things were going so well. It does seem hard. But what can one do.

The remaining pages of the journal remained blank. It was not a cheery way to begin a day, even less so after what could only be described as a life-affirming evening. As I closed the journal, I resolved to buy a padded envelope and send the volume to Beatrice Lane, Phyllis Donaldson's niece.

As I sat, thoughtfully sipping my coffee and feeling intensely alive, I hoped Mrs. Donaldson had been well cared for. My curiosity about her death did not extend to telephoning the niece; but as I sat, blessedly alone, a question began to formulate itself. In an earlier entry Phyllis Donaldson spoke of an art deco cocktail shaker she intended to let Jonathan sell on consignment, but she made no mention of other china or silver. Having seen both a Georgian tankard and pink-bordered china in Jonathan's apartment, I could not stifle a gnawing suspicion that these might be the missing items about which the niece had telephoned. Were Jonathan to have had a key to Phyllis Donaldson's apartment, now mine, could he not have helped himself to whatever he wanted?

I seldom read detective novels. Plot-driven fiction, peopled by two-dimensional figures, bores me silly. Somewhere in the Deleted File in my brain reside any number of unsolved plots, detective novels begun only to be discarded for any number of reasons. Yet were I to construct an outline for a story, what better premise than a lonely older woman, an attractive but unscrupulous younger man, and an apartment filled with valuable objects about which she is indifferent but he covets.

In short, did Jonathan simply walk off with Phyllis Danaldson's possessions, or did she, at some point during her decline, give them away? At the moment I seriously doubted I would ever know. Jonathan was nothing if not shrewd; furthermore, it was none of my business.

Supposing, just supposing, I called the niece, Beatrice Lane, to tell her I thought I had located the missing china and silver, what then? Would she be sufficiently curious to come to Montreal to investigate? I would most certainly be involved, with the result that I would end up on bad terms with my neighbour across the hall. Perhaps the best course of action was to do nothing.

The telephone rang. The chance of a call being for me was slight, but I answered anyway.

"Did you make it back to Diana's unscathed?" Sean's naturally resonant voice hummed down the line.

"Absolutely. The Armenian cab driver told me all about his new granddaughter. I took my cue and asked if he had a photo. Wrong question; he had a small album. But his delight was contagious. Diana was asleep, and by the time I awoke this morning she had gone out. I didn't even have to fib."

Sean laughed. "I really called to find out when you are going to invite me to dinner so I can see your new place."

"As soon as Craig leaves. He said he was going to New York for a bit. I'm to have lunch with him today, so I'll learn more about his plans. Then I shall ignore the injunction I learned as a girl, to wit: that she should never under any circumstances telephone a man for a date — and give you a call. I'm not used to the kitchen, so it may well be a comfort food meal."

"The food is secondary. I would like to see the apartment — and you; that goes without saying. So I'll wait to hear from you."

I put down the receiver with wry amusement. Some things do not change. Not an ungenerous man, Sean had always kept a kind of mental ledger of accounts receivable. If he took me out to dinner it became my turn to provide a meal for him. Because of my young son, I generally shopped and cooked at Sean's flat. A letter sent demanded a letter in return. He kept track of who and, more important, who did not send him Christmas and birthday cards. How much more so for Christmas and birthday gifts.

His was a mindset designed to guarantee an almost constant state of pique, as few could rise to his level of punctiliousness. I overcompensated by showering him with small, inexpensive gifts — soap, tinned paté, or anything from a stationary store. But I was older now, wiser I would like to think, and less determined to please. However, it was definitely in the cards to show him my new home, so once I had bought myself a meatloaf pan I would be all set.

The next two phone calls were for Diana, and I dutifully took down messages. My cousin lived under constant siege from volunteer workers, confident that if they could engage Diana Hamilton for their cause, then it would prosper.

When the phone rang again I decided to let the answering service take the message, that is until I saw my own telephone number on the display screen.

"Craig?"

"Venerable mother. Are we having lunch today?"

"I hope so. We still have much catching up to do. I feel as if you belong to an earlier life: the B.M. rather than the A.M."

"Sounds rude."

"It isn't. Before Move and After Move. I'm just beginning to come to grips with the fact that Victoria is far, far away."

"I guess. Shall I swing by and pick you up?"

"Why not. There are several places to eat within strolling distance."

We agreed on a time. Craig is always punctual; I greeted him dressed and ready to go. Diana had not yet returned, so

I left a note saying I would pick up the wherewithal for dinner. Life is easier for those who pay their dues. Not a bad epitaph for a tombstone, but I wanted to be cremated, like Walter. Ashes to ashes, dust to dust; and why waste good green space on another grave.

∽

As part of his ongoing campaign against professional victims, my late husband Walter used to ask me, "Can I spoil your day and tell you some good news?" Bad news gets around fast, almost as fast as a confession made in strictest confidence. A piece of good news can rest unreported until it has passed its sell-by date, unless of course the disclosure of success will bring on an attack of acute envy in the person seated across the lunch table.

My lunch with Craig almost capsized from the weight of good news, namely, that he had definitely decided to abandon the West Coast and move back east. With his customary tact and timing he waited for the right occasion to make his announcement; the end result was that I would not have to face five hours on Air Canada in order to visit my son. The details of what else we discussed fade into the realization that he would no longer be a continent away. I had no intention of turning into a smother-mother, expecting him for regular meals and performing endless small services for which I could demand emotional returns. Quite simply,

I like the idea of geographical proximity to my only son. *Voilà tout.*

So pleased was I with the news that a casual remark made as we left the restaurant registered only as a blip on my mindscreen.

"By the way, Louise, you can move back to the apartment anytime after tomorrow. Jonathan has offered me his guest-room; I'll stay with him when I get back from New York. That way I won't be underfoot, and you won't be pressured into buying stuff you don't really like for the spare room."

"A bed is a bed. I had planned to shop tomorrow. I hate to think of you bunking in with the neighbour because your feckless welfare mother can't afford furniture."

Craig laughed. "Not to worry. I'll be just across the hall. You can still feed me from time to time." He glanced at his watch. "I have to hurry. I have an appointment. You'll get home safely?"

"I expect so — unless I happen to be kidnapped, drugged, and sold into white slavery. And I think the prospect of that happening on Crescent Street is slight. Call me before you leave."

The afternoon shimmered with haze as I walked back to Diana's building. It was only after walking a few blocks that I began to experience a feeling of unease, slight but nagging. I did not like the idea of Craig staying with Jonathan. My misgiving did not have a name or a shape and rested on nothing more than a mistrust of my neighbour. I did not really like the man, but that in itself was no reason why Craig should not use his guestroom.

On the plus side I would be pleased to get back to my own place, away from Diana and the obligations attendant on being a guest. Also I would be able to invite Sean for dinner and a little bumpity-bump. I might even attempt something more adventurous than a meatloaf, a daube perhaps, nothing that would require split-second timing. That would come when Sean and I had worked out some sort of understanding. Were we to graduate to an affair, then, and only then, would I undertake veal scaloppini.

If I had one bit of sound advice to offer to younger women it would be not to waste your best recipes on early dates. It has been said the way to a man's heart is through his stomach. As any surgeon will tell you, the way to a man's heart is through his ribcage, but keep a few good meals in reserve. Sex is usually enough for the early weeks, but a good Beef Wellington can help one through a bad patch.

As it turned out, I missed Craig's call as I had gone out to buy something for dinner. Since I was committed to one more night at Diana's, I had volunteered to cook. To be fair to my cousin, she was prepared to address the stove, but I chatted her down. For Diana food is fuel; she eats because her body requires nourishment. This nutritional bottom line does not lead to creative cuisine. So long as the piece of meat is not still throbbing, the vegetables are boiled to chewable consistency, and the potatoes are baked all the way through, Diana is perfectly satisfied. In a silver-plated cruet caddy sit bottles of sauce: HP, Mint, Worcestershire, all imported from the U.K., whose purpose is to add a gourmet touch to an otherwise boarding-school meal.

Even though I make no grandiose claims about my own cooking, I still prefer my meals to Diana's, with the result that my volunteering to make dinner was tinged with self-interest. In this vale of tears, whose motives are abolutely pure? In any event, I was basting chicken breasts when Craig telephoned to say he was indeed off to New York for about five days, meaning I could move back to Queen's Court any time I liked.

Ordinarily, Diana sits at the kitchen table sipping a weak scotch and soda while I cook. Not being a temperamental chef, I don't have to be alone in order to bond with my culinary muse, but tonight Diana chose to watch television while I puttered in the kitchen. I did not mind the solitude as I was trying to decide if I should rent a car for a day and drive out to the IKEA and IDOMO warehouse stores to buy furniture for the second bedroom, or whether I should wait until Diana took delivery of her new Lexus sedan sometime next week. Then she could chauffeur me.

I wanted to furnish the room before Craig returned from New York so he would not be obliged to stay with Jonathan.

Even by proxy I did not want to be obligated to my neighbour. At the same time I did not want to rush into buying furniture I did not truly like merely to accommodate Craig for a few days. After all, what he needed was a box spring and mattress which could sit on the floor until I found the bed I wanted.

With just such idle thoughts did I occupy myself as I basted the chicken, rinsed the rice, and made a vinaigrette for the salad. Neither Diana nor I eat dessert, so that was not an issue. Over dinner Diana was uncharacteristically quiet.

"This chicken is delicious, Louise. Will you share the secret?"

"I baste the breasts with vermouth and lemon juice, quite often. Otherwise they dry out."

"I must try it sometime."

We ate in silence for a while.

"I'll be moving back to my apartment tomorrow," I said, serving salad onto Coalport plates, a wedding present Diana had heretofore considered too good to use for everyday. Ordinarily she would have made some sort of observation about "Keeping up with the Joneses;" but tonight she kept silent and toyed with her food. The topic of my dinner with Sean never came up.

"Do you know when your new car will be delivered?"

"Next week sometime. I'll have to call."

"Would you like more of anything?"

"No thanks. It's awfully good, but I don't seem to have much appetite."

Diana helped me to clear away, after which we settled down to watch a movie on television.

❧

Since it was not the first time in my life I had watched Bette Davis go bravely blind, I sneaked away during one of the commercial breaks and telephoned Sean. I had every intention of asking him over for a meal, but — those impure motives again — maybe he had access to a car, or knew someone who might be prepared to drive me to the outskirts of town. My motives were not purely selfish. Walter and I had leased a car in Victoria, but he did most of the driving. I used the vehicle for short errands around town, but on those rare occasions we took the car by ferry to the mainland Walter always drove. Far from feeling belittled, I was only too happy to turn over the keys and the responsibility. To tell the truth, I felt a little apprehensive about driving in and around Montreal, a much larger city than Victoria. Since my arrival I had rediscovered the Gallic insouciance that informs the local urban traffic. The wary pedestrian must look both ways before venturing to cross on a green light, while only the admittedly suicidal would attempt a pedestrian crosswalk. I have taken cabs, cowering in the back seat and wishing that St. Christopher had not been discredited as the patron saint of travellers. Not even the seemingly impregnable bulk of the number twenty-four bus could completely allay my fears. Consequently, I found myself reluctant to slide behind the wheel of an unfamiliar car and head out into the cheerful chaos of Montreal traffic. There had to be another way.

I caught Sean at home.

"Louise, what's up?"

"Craig has left for New York. I'm at Diana's for tonight, but tomorrow I return to the old homestead. Would y'all care to come by for some grub?'

"Sho' 'nuff."

"It won't be elaborate. I have to move back and straighten up the place."

"I have a better idea. Why don't I bring my Chinese take-out menu? No fuss. No muss."

"Only if you will let me pay."

"It would be ungentlemanly of me to argue. What o'clock?"

"Anytime after six. I will ply you with strong drink while we decide. I don't like the really spicy food. 'Speecy-spicey,' as the Swedish chef would say."

"Neither do I. I dislike all cuisine that makes my eyes water."

"Then we are agreed."

I returned to find Bette Davis groping her way up to the bedroom for the last time and Diana asleep in her chair. As I switched channels she jolted awake.

"I must have nodded off."

Why did I know she would say that?

∽

"OH, AUNTIE EM, there's no place like home!" How good it was to be back in my own house, unfurnished though it might be. Craig had left the apartment immaculate, the bed freshly made up, the bathroom gleaming. I am by nature tidy, but not obsessively so. Craig, on the other had inherited a neatness gene that had him picking up his room at four years old. If it ain't broke, don't fix it. Needless to say I did not discourage this trait, which made my life as working mother so much easier.

For a few moments I thought I might go out to shop so I could cook dinner for Sean, but the thought evaporated with little resistance. When had I last eaten Chinese takeout? Also I wanted to spend time with Sean rather than chained to an unfamiliar stove in a kitchen I had yet to learn. Instead I decided to make hot little cheese whatnots to serve with drinks.

To tell the truth, I was flying blind, which I suppose is another way of saying I did not know exactly what I wanted or where I was headed. Fanning the flames of an old romance can be risky. Is it possible to turn today's meat loaf into yesterday's *filet mignon*? Did I really hope to? I am certainly not the first to have observed that seldom do two people desire the same things from a relationship. One may want romance, open fire, and *La Bohème* on the stereo; while the other wants companionship, someone prepared to help build a deck and lose gracefully at Scrabble. One may hanker after the kind of randy sex that isolates; the other a warm body to curl around for uninterrupted sleep. Some men want to be challenged in a marriage, others stroked and endlessly reassured. This woman wants Prince Charming, all courtesy and deference; that one fancies a bit of rough trade, pancake makeup over bruises and steamy reconciliations.

Then there is the endless problem of money. The green-eyed monster may indeed be jealousy, but more often he turns out to be an ominous presence seated on a stack of unpaid bills.

I got lucky when I married Walter. Most of the building blocks we needed for a civilized life came from the same Lego set. For the rest we were prepared to compromise. I may not have been willing to help build the deck, but I did lose at Scrabble, never more than three games in a row. And I played killer Canasta. We had our share of good sex, largely before we decided to get married; but isn't that often the case.

My mother's generation talked of men who "strayed," meaning they screwed other women on the Q.T. If Walter strayed he covered his tracks, and I found the logistics of an affair too demanding. The plotting, stage-managing, synchronizing of watches and alibis defeated me. Fidelity was a whole lot easier. Also, with few notable exceptions, my first husband being one, sex rarely lives up to expectation. The idea of sex, the anticipation and longing, all too often outstrips the untidy and frequently comical act. Yet whenever people, gay or straight, tell of a sexual encounter, it is always "great." Who will admit to having dull, unsatisfactory, or inconsequential sex. The domain of sexual narrative does not allow for premature ejaculation, limp dicks, dry vaginas, or simple indifference. I cannot help thinking that were there as much tumescence, lubricity, as many multiple, simultaneous orgasms as song and story would have it, then the United Nations would go out of business.

All this idle speculation did not pinpoint what I hoped for from Sean. Good Sex? Check. A presentable escort? Check. A man with whom I can converse? Check. Someone old enough to understand what I find funny? Check. Someone with whom I could really let down barriers? Perhaps. Someone with whom to totter into the sunset? Pass.

Now it was time to shower and put on something that telegraphed alluring and available. Funny, but I've never come across that particular subsection in the L.L. Bean catalogue. Then there were the little cheese whatnots to prepare. Then again, perhaps not. They blunt appetite, and I had a tin of cashews on the shelf.

೧

After doing my face I tried on a pair of tapered slacks, then took a long, hard, uncompromising look at myself in the full-length mirror on the closet door in my dressing room. Although I have not put on weight since I married Walter (well, maybe ten pounds) my contours have shifted. Were it not for the force of gravity, the world as we know it would fly apart, but that particular pull is not kind to women in their late middle years. Off came the slacks, to be replaced by a long black hostess skirt. This change offered two advantages: concealed were the slightly saddlebag thighs; also I did not have to wear pantyhose. A matching black turtleneck showed off a jade disc on a thong, rather too Sixties for my taste, but I suspected that turbulent decade remained Sean's spiritual home.

The final touch was to splash on 4711, the German cologne with the illegible blue and gold label. I realize it is generally considered a man's aftershave, but something about my skin chemistry makes 4711 smell quite exotic. And I have never been the type for those heavy, sweet perfumes that clog the elevator.

Sean arrived promptly at six. "I know punctuality is supposed to be the virtue of the bored," he began after kissing me lightly on the lips, "but I assure you I am free of ennui." His left hand held a maroon bag emblazoned with the SAQ logo in gold. "Something to warm the premises."

I expected the bag to hold red wine, his colour of choice, but was pleasantly surprised to find a bottle of single-malt scotch.

"Very generous I must say."

Sean nodded an acknowledgement, but his attention focused on the apartment. "I must say, Louise, this is awfully nice — not nice; I detest that word, but handsome and spacious."

"Would you like a drink before the tour?"

"No, tour first."

It is always interesting, for me at least, to see my residence through the eyes of someone else. Sean prowled through the apartment, silently appraising the spacious master bedroom with its dressing room and bath *en suite*, as grandly described in the ads. The second bedroom really gave him pause.

"I had no idea your place was so large. For a second bedroom this is huge. You could sublet the closet."

"Empty rooms always appear larger, but these older buildings do have generous spaces. Had I known the size of the rooms I was going to inhabit I might have brought more furniture from Victoria. But I had a chance to sell, and I wanted to unload . . ."

I could tell Sean was not listening. He stood in the middle of the floor, bathed in late afternoon light from a large window that overlooked Sherbrooke Street. It was a handsome room, possibly better proportioned than the master bedroom; but the second bathroom also served as house washroom, and there was no adjoining dressing room. In my house in Victoria I did not have a dressing room, and the closets here are so generous my modest wardrobe looks forlorn.

Sean gave the kitchen (basic pullman, but convenient) the once-over while I poured drinks. Then he carried his glass into the spare bedroom for one last look.

"Did you bring the takeout menu?" I inquired. "Perhaps we should think of ordering in case delivery is slow."

After the usual huddle over the brochure we decided on egg rolls, beef with snow-pea pods, ginger chicken, honey-lemon shrimp, and chicken-fried rice. In spite of his lean physique Sean liked to chow down; I doubted there would be leftovers for my lunch tomorrow.

While we waited for our order to arrive we proceeded to tie one on. It was good to have what is euphemistically called "a couple of drinks" with someone who truly enjoys his whiskey. I don't believe for a moment that drinking alone leads to perdition and the primrose path, not necessarily in that order; but when I drink alone I drink less. One scotch and water lasts a long time, the glass at my elbow while I read, more of a companion than a crutch. Diana nurses a glass of wine as though it were the last drink in the world and considers me a tosspot for liking whiskey. Consequently I enjoyed having that extra drink, even though a small voice in my head warned me I would be sorry tomorrow. At the moment tomorrow seemed like a different dimension in time as I knocked back the whiskey like a contract player in a B movie.

Sean was most definitely "on." As a retired professor, one who had opted for early retirement, he could string words together into sentences without verbal fillers: "like/you know/sort of." He could begin the answer to a question without "well," followed by a pause. As we sat, talking about everything and nothing, I could sense a faint but agreeable sexual tension, the feeling that we both understood the evening would end in bed. We had passed the age for the pantomime of love, the locked glances, brushed hands, little squeezes — those small gestures of reassurance that suggest the ephemeral is forever.

What I also enjoyed, furthermore without a twinge of conscience, was the realization that the Widow Bingham had put aside her widow's weeds, in spite of the fact I was dressed head to toe in black. I also understood there is a widows' lobby, of which Diana is a charter member, that would censure me for sleeping with a man so soon after my husband's death. A period must elapse, one measuring itself in years, not months, during which I must tend the sacred flame and forego pleasures of the flesh, notably scotch followed by sex. I have yet to be convinced that virtue as denial is motivated less by sanctity than simple envy. I am not getting it, so why should you. I also knew for certain that Walter would have been the last person in the world to suggest I put my life on hold because his had ended.

The best way to keep a man in a good mood is to massage his ego without making it obvious. Feminine wiles have not gone away; they have gone underground. If anyone today carried on like Scarlett O'Hara at Seven Oaks she would be laughed out of the room and pelted with Colonel Sanders's southern fried chicken. To this day I am sorry that Melanie didn't slap her bowlegged, but then I have always disliked manipulative women. The fact remains that I did ask Sean whether he had a project going now that he no longer taught. What man dislikes talking about himself?

"As a matter of fact, Louise, I'm thinking seriously of doing a book, a survey of Eighteenth-Century Literature from, say, Dryden to Byron, or the beginnings of Romanticism."

"Hasn't it already been done?"

"To be sure. But I'm thinking of a college text, a critical anthology for undergraduate courses. A steady seller rather than a best-seller. I've taught the material for years, but I never found a comprehensive textbook that I was comfortable with."

"Why don't you write a thriller and make some real money?"

"Easier said than done. We write the books we can, not those we should. Otherwise every single volume would be a best-seller. *Plants Without Pesticides*: soon to be a minor motion picture!"

I laughed out loud. A great many things appear to be outrageously funny when you expect to get laid. I would be hard put to imagine a duller project than an Eighteenth-Century critical anthology: *Absalom and Achitophel*, *The Rape of the Lock*, nuggets of Dr. Johnson, fragments of Boswell's *Life of Johnson*, excerpts from Fanny Burney's Journals and Diaries, perhaps a chapter or two of *Evelina*. Would Byron really make the cut? I wish somebody would undertake to make the nineteen-sixties comprehensible to "the common reader," but now was not the time to douse enthusiasm.

The arrival of our food changed the subject.

"My purse is in the bedroom," I said; but Sean raised his hands, palms facing out. "No. Let me get this."

"But we agreed it was to be on me. I don't even have to cook."

"No, no. You provided the drinks and cashews. I'll provide the cash. Small joke there."

"Minimal." But I laughed anyway. I could tell Sean was in a good mood, and a good mood leads to better sex. But I still ate three of the six honey shrimp. Scarlett O'Hara would have insisted Sean eat all the shrimp, but I gave him his head on the ginger chicken and fried rice.

I was right. A good mood leads to good sex. Walter used to say fucking is like playing the harmonium; you're always pulling or pushing or pumping — and you're a little bit relieved when it's all over. A few drinks helped to banish those programmed inhibitions, and both of us felt more comfortable the second time around. Sean remembered the small intimacies I particularly enjoyed and, not to labour the point, we enjoyed a Grade-A fuck.

Between the scotch and the food and post-coital lassitude, I was more than content to lie beside Sean without speaking. Pillow talk is for the young. Sean put his lean but well-defined arm around my shoulders as we lay together like two halves of an indenture.

"I have an idea," he began slowly, almost tentatively. "Are you up to dealing with an idea?"

"If it's not too taxing, and with absolutely no mental arithmetic or, worse still, algebra."

"No, nothing like that." He shifted his leg so that it lay, not unpleasantly, against mine. "I was wondering if you would consider renting me your spare room."

In spite of myself I stiffened, only slightly, but enough to be felt.

Sean gave my shoulders a squeeze. "I know the idea comes as a surprise," he continued, his voice low and soothing, as though he was speaking to a nervous child; "but there might be advantages for both of us. I told you I had to move, so why not turn a negative into a plus. I could arrange the second bedroom as both sleeping space and office; there's plenty of room — and you could use my furniture, whatever you want of it, to fill in the gaps."

In my somnolent state the magnitude of what Sean was proposing only began to take shape. The prospect of a lodger-lover hadn't even remotely suggested itself, mainly, I suppose, because I did not want one. Trying to keep the agitation out of my voice I asked, "But what about all your books?"

"I plan to get rid of a great number. And there's plenty of wall space in the spare room for shelves. Also, there's an alcove in your entrance hall that is perfect for shelves. You will have books of your own, and I can use the rest of the space." As Sean warmed to his subject his voice rose in volume. "You said yourself that you have nothing to put in your basement locker. I could store cartons of books down there."

By now wide awake, I found it was all I could do not to jump out of bed and pull on a robe, the better to combat the giant seduction in progress.

"How would we cope with meals?"

"We'd share expenses for food. Remember; I'll be paying you board, so that will cut down on your own expenses. You're a wonderful cook; I should know. And you know what they say about people who live alone getting into bad eating habits. What incentive is there to cook just for yourself?"

"So I get to make dinner for two."

"Only when you want to. I know my way around a kitchen, only I don't cook half as well as you."

Somehow the compliment failed to raise a glow of gratitude. Was I being manipulated? Yes! I decided a trip to the bathroom was in order, less for hygiene than escape. I didn't need to pee, and were I to conceive at this point in my life I would first have to be visited by an angel bearing a lily. But I turned on the taps and made official noises. My robe, a slippery synthetic number, ideal for travel, hung on the door. I pulled it on before venturing out.

"Would you like a highball, or a beer?" I asked, anxious to change the subject. Sean did not reply, as he was not in the room. Seconds later he padded into the bedroom, having used the second bathroom. I repeated the question as he slid once more into my bed.

"Not at the moment, thanks."

"Sean," I began as I sat on the far side of the bed, "what happens if I want to entertain?"

"I'll stay in my room, or go out. No sweat."

"And if you want to have someone in?"

"I'm not big on entertaining at home. If I should, you'd always be welcome to join us."

"I see. Now, what will the neighbours think? Won't there be an ugly rumour about — my ugly roomer? Little joke there."

Sean managed a polite laugh. "I think we are old enough to deal with the gossip, although who would waste time gossiping about us I cannot imagine." He rolled over and put his hand on my knee. "You're not going to get sick of me, Louise; I guarantee that. I plan to spend a good part of next year in England, travelling and doing research for my book. You can use my room as your guest room — and you won't have the bother of furnishing."

My reluctance must have been palpable, as Sean sat up. "Don't worry about the money; I'll pay my share whether I use the room or not." He smiled and lowered his voice. "Now why don't you come back to bed?"

For just a moment I fought down the impulse to throw my head back and howl like a wolf. The feeling passed. I also realized that whatever sex I would enjoy with Sean must take place between this moment and the one when I admitted that under no circumstances could I live with him.

I slid off the robe and let it slide to the floor, just like the heroine of a medieval romance or Arthurian legend. Beautiful damsels were forever stepping out of robes and into pools, or springs, or fountains, leaving their gowns in a heap on the ground. Either they wore wrinkle-free fabrics or else, hidden behind the arras, lurked a maid with an ironing board. I did not have to worry about my discarded dressing gown, since a garbage compactor could not crush the sleazy fabric. Snuggling once again against Sean, I allowed hope to banish experience. Men in their sixties are not as a rule given to encores. In short order the breathing I heard did not emerge as aspirated gasps but rather as deep, regular exhalations. Sean was asleep.

The same could not be said for me. I had just been handed a major dose of insomnia, and the deep breathing beside me only served to underline my wakefulness. Once more I swung myself out of bed and pulled on my robe, more bargain basement than *Belle Dame Sans Merci*. Wandering into the kitchen I poured myself a glass of water and sat in the one comfortable chair to consider my options. There was not much to mull over.

Perhaps naively I had imagined a tidy little scenario in which Sean played an important part. What could be more pleasant for a woman in my situation than to have a straight man in the picture, furthermore one who was prepared to steer his heterosexual impulses in my direction. I could foresee a series of dinners, movies, the occasional concert or gallery opening, possibly even travel, all in the company of a man I genuinely liked, whose company I enjoyed, and who had my number in bed. I did not want to own him, only borrow him one or two nights a week. I certainly did not love him, for which I felt hugely relieved. At one point, long ago, I thought perhaps I did; but my sense of self-preservation came to the rescue. Somehow I realized that I would be relegated to the intellectual equivalent of walking two paces behind. To rebel would have thrown the relationship off its one true course, with a resulting emotional collision.

I did not want to be Sean's landlady. Nothing kills intimacy more quickly than familiarity. To see him unshaven and borderline cranky in the morning must soon banish whatever magic, mystery, or rapture that we, at our age, could muster. I did not want to be seen uncombed, minus lipstick, barefoot, and belted into unpressed cotton or terrycloth, depending on the weather.

Even though I am first to admit interior decoration is not salvation, I did not want Sean's Salvation Army furniture cluttering my apartment. For Sean a chair was a chair; a table, a table; and a desk just that. How these pieces of furniture appeared to the naked eye did not matter so long as they served their basic purpose. A wooden crate that once held twelve bottles of club soda is not my idea of a nightstand. A trunk, even waxed and polished, makes a cumbersome coffee table; and his living room suite, bought at a fire sale, is upholstered in hideous ochre and black tartan. I once thought this indifference to surroundings admirable, strong evidence that Sean's preoccupations were not with the mundane. Now I realize it is merely another form of laziness. My soul does not cry out for Tudor, Directoire, or Second Empire; but I draw the line at brick-and-board shelves, lamps made from wine bottles, and curtains that began life as bedding.

As I absently sipped my glass of water I remembered how Sean used to help me in the kitchen. Leaning against the doorjamb, holding a glass of wine or a highball, he would offer to make salad. This gesture of infinite largesse meant monopolizing the sink and most of the counter space in the small room. Whatever I was doing went on hold unless, as I might point out, the meat would scorch or the sauce separate were I to be interrupted. He would shrug and return to his book, leaving me to deal with salad. To have offered was the equivalent of having done. On occasion, having steered the casserole into the oven, I might suggest the kitchen was all his. He would then manage to look infinitely puzzled, as though I had suggested he scale the façade of the Sun Life Building, then ask if we really needed salad. Most of the time I took the hint and made it myself. I was younger then and more anxious to please. On occasion I called his bluff and served the lasagne, Swiss steak, or swordfish by itself. Invariably he would remark we had no salad to refresh the palate. In short, I had absolutely no intention of drifting into a situation where my superior skill as cook meant I would be expected to make dinner. Neither a borrower nor a lender, a cook nor a landlady be.

The final caveat arose from the easy assumption that he could move in and out of my life as he pleased. So you like having me around? Sorry, I'm off to the U.K. for six months. In the meantime you can store my stuff, forward my mail, and — Oh, would you mind picking up my dry cleaning. Petty though it might appear, I could not avoid just a touch of rancour to realize that Sean's seemingly spontaneous generosity: the bottle of scotch, his paying for dinner twice in a row, sprang from a core of self-interest. Did even his deft and satisfying lovemaking serve a larger purpose, that of making himself more desirable in my life? I did not know; I would never attempt to learn; nor would I ever be completely free of suspicion.

The package was so unappealing I could almost have laughed. But the hour had grown late; my bed had been colonized by a man not my husband and with whom I had not expected to sleep; and I knew, beyond all doubt, that once I said no to Sean's proposal I was also saying so-long. To admit I felt sad might be too strong, but I could not escape an overpowering sense of regret. The status quo would have been ideal, but I have read Spenser's *Cantos of Mutability*. The only constant is change.

I returned to the bedroom and once more removed my robe. This time I folded it carefully to drape over the folding bridge chair, borrowed from Diana, which served as my night table. Who was I to find fault with a soft-drink crate?

I fell into a light, troubled slumber. When I awoke, Sean was gone.

6

When I first realized the bed beside me was empty I felt a twinge of regret. A spot of early morning sex was always a good way to begin a day. As Walter grew older, whatever interest he had in K.S. (Kama Sutra, our code for a tumble) was at its most pronounced in the morning. As a result I had grown used to morning sex, even though I prefer to be wide awake. But, as the poet cautions us, "Gather ye rosebuds," etc.

Yet as I tugged on my badly battered, cotton-polyester *peignoir* one more time I felt a bit relieved to have the place to myself. A note on the borrowed dining table in Sean's neat, precise calligraphy claimed a forgotten dentist appointment. One excuse is as good as another; I suspect the real reason for his early departure was to give me breathing space and time to mull over his proposition.

If anything, I felt more resolved this morning not to let Sean into my apartment and, by extension, my life than I had felt last night. As the coffee machine gurgled cheerfully away, I luxuriated in the empty space. The idea of entering into a sort of partnership in which I would come out second best on every level filled me with dismay. At the same time I understood there would be benefits, not least of which would be companionship, someone with whom to discuss events of the day, to share a recent joke, to listen when a sympathetic ear was needed. In spite of Sean's tacit assumption that women occupied a lower rank on the Great Chain of Being, he was essentially a decent man, never violent nor rude, essentially kind. His defects, if such they could legitimately be called, sprang from the kind of masculine self-absorption endemic to the species. There were times when my husband Walter moved in such an impermeable bubble of solipsism, especially concerning his garden, that I felt as if the English I normally spoke was a foreign language. My first husband, Serge, actually asked me questions; furthermore, he listened to my answers. He also had six-pack abs long before they became *de rigueur* among dating males. But that was decades ago, and dwelling on past happiness is a fail-safe recipe for present misery.

I had been married twice, raised a son, helped raise a stepdaughter, had my share of lovers, and survived menopause without jumping off a bridge. I have dealt with men, made accommodations of which I did not approve, and emerged as a widow in her sixties. I confess I like the idea of a man in my life, but only on my terms. I will no longer sell myself short for a stiff prick, or a semi-stiff one that requires a lot of fluffing. My biggest concern was how to turn Sean away without turning him off. Maybe I couldn't, but under no circumstances would I allow him to take over my life.

Ten A.M. found me walking into the nearest department store, where I bought a double bed for the spare room. Next I bought sheets and pillowcases in ochre and burnt sienna, very masculine I thought. I also ordered a quilted mattress pad. My mother had been punctilious about mattress pads, convinced as she was that around four A.M. men would become suddenly incontinent and women unexpectedly begin to menstruate. I chose a pair of acrylic blankets, which the saleswoman convinced me were both warm and washable. Finally, in another department, I purchased what I would have called a dressing gown but what the saleswoman insisted was a housecoat. The rich cerulean blue threw my silver hair and blue eyes into relief, so I ignored the Dry Clean Only label and handed over my credit card. Besides, the saleswoman was Gallic and charming and obliging. How could I disappoint her?

As I left the department store and stood, while the seedy, shoddy, vital, and varied panorama of St. Catherine Street swirled past, I realized I had crossed my own personal

Rubicon with Sean. My way or the highway, and why the hell had I waited so long to reach this point. But, as we say in Quebec, "*Mieux vaut tard que jamais.*"

Not only was I pleased with my purchases, both their real and symbolic presence, I also felt the surge of adrenaline that comes from having bested an opponent, in this instance the female who had sold me the bed. Unlike the delightful saleswoman who cajoled me into choosing the dressing gown/housecoat/*robe de chambre*, the wench who had been set loose in the furniture department bore a chip on her shoulder the size of Place Ville-Marie. It took me no little time to flag her down, although I appeared to be the only customer. At once I realized she carried a great deal of what the young call "attitude." Under a minimal skirt, way too short for business attire, she wore a leg brace, one of those moulded plastic affairs held in place by giant velcro straps, the whole in a particularly unattractive shade of blue. The contraption stretched from the middle of her thigh to just above the ankle and obliged her to walk like Quaismodo. An ankle-length skirt would have concealed the contraption and added immeasurably to her appearance; at the same time it would have undermined her determined look of passive aggression, further enhanced by hair badly in need of washing and a face innocent of makeup.

She stood, just out of my sight line without speaking. When I inquired about the bed she asked me, quite rudely

I thought, if I spoke French. I do but I lied, obliging her to switch into what turned out to be fluent English. We proceeded in businesslike fashion to conclude the transaction, and I brought up the question of delivery. It seems that tomorrow was delivery day in my part of the city, but it was too late to notify the warehouse; I would have to wait until next week. It takes two to play chicken. I announced that next week was too late, that my son was coming to stay in two days, and that I needed the bed now. Shifting her weight, she leaned heavily on the desk for support and repeated there was nothing she could do; the warehouse required forty-eight-hours' notice. I observed, almost casually, that I had gone to high school with the manager of the store and was just on my way up to his office to say hello. As I gazed into the middle distance I saw her straighten up, remove the supporting hand from the edge of the desk, and reach for the telephone. Would tomorrow morning be all right? Tomorrow morning would be quite satisfactory, thank you.

Then to encounter the charming woman who sold me the upscale bathrobe? She could have sold me something trimmed in marabou. Whatever happened to marabou? It looked sensational on Jean Harlow, but those sleeves get in the way when you are trying to scramble eggs.

Although I had fibbed about not speaking French, I did not lie about having gone to school with the manager. I have not seen him since graduation, and were I to walk into his office I doubt he would recognize me. My stated intention of visiting his office had been an on-the-spot fabrication, but there are times when we must all airbrush the truth.

A more recent addition to St. Catherine Street, one which I did not applaud, was the large number of panhandlers, beggars by any other name. At least Canadian mendicants do not thrust diseased limbs under your nose in a bid for sympathy. Although I would like to believe I have freed myself from the dogmas of formal religion, I still find myself susceptible to the puritanical, protestant ethic, in particular as regards beggars. I am more inclined to give to someone who offers something in return, a cheap ball-point pen, a candy bar, or some form of entertainment. Anyone prepared to stand on a street corner playing the recorder, or the fiddle, or even percussive spoons, has a superior claim on my dollar coin than a churl thrusting out a baseball cap from a seated position. My advice to beggars: always stand when soliciting. Your mark is upright, and a seated person is higher on the pecking order. In effect the person in the superior social position is asking the inferior for money. It is also difficult to make eye contact when seated, and eyeballing the passing pedestrian brings in the loonies.

As I window-shopped along St. Catherine I handed out the four dollars I had transferred from my shoulder bag to my pocket. About to turn up towards Sherbrooke Street I was accosted by one last panhandler, a rubby who looked as though he had not eaten in days. Reluctant to bring out my wallet, I remembered I had a candy bar, one of those quick-energy snacks that virtuously lists the ingredients on the wrapper. I dropped the foil-wrapped bar into his outstretched baseball cap.

He glared at me. "I'd prefer cash."

"I'm sure you would," I replied primly, "but beggars can't be choosers."

So pleased was I to have been given the opportunity to utter that tired platitude in context that I would willingly have given him money, but he had already turned his back and was shuffling away.

As I entered my apartment I experienced another of those small epiphanies of solitude, a feeling of pleasure so intense — that this space was mine all mine — I would have liked to turn to someone and exclaim over the fact. Then, with a smile, I realized having an audience would negate the cause. After putting down the bag of overpriced items picked up at a convenience store, I noticed the message light flickering on my phone. The outside world clamoured to be let in, and my initial euphoria began to evaporate as I punched in the retrieval code.

My heart leaped down when Diana's voice proceeded to deliver one of those messages that manage to make the listener feel if not exactly guilty then at least vaguely apprehensive. A recital was to take place the following Sunday afternoon, a noted tenor having agreed to donate his services to help raise funds for one of the local orchestras. Diana had agreed to take a block of seats and forgotten to mark down the date in her calendar. Would I like to go and perhaps invite someone? She had taken ten tickets and so far found only three people besides herself who were free on that afternoon. (At this point I began to regret not having one of those answering tapes that said you had one minute to leave your name, number, and a brief message.) Diana's voice continued relentlessly to explain that since she was inviting people at the last minute she felt obliged to have them back after the concert for drinks and enough finger foods to stand for supper. She was having the affair catered, as usual. It did seem an awful shame to let the tickets — fifth-row-centre — go to waste. It was to be a lovely recital: Schubert, Fauré, and something Spanish — de Falla? Nin? She couldn't be sure. And the usual operatic bits, even though she didn't much care for operatic arias sung with piano accompaniment. In any event, could I call her as soon as possible to let her know how many tickets I wanted, and of course I and my party would be expected back at her flat for drinks and whatnots. Well, that about covered it, although why she neglected to mark down the date on her calendar she'll never know. She must have been having a senior moment. Call soon.

I put down the receiver feeling as though I had just been mugged. Yet the basic invitation, a recital for me and my friends followed by drinks and catered snacks, did not sound that bad. There was a good chance Craig would be back from

New York by then, and I would invite Sean. I knew he loved singing, although he could be a bit snooty about opera, which he found obvious. On the other hand I find a little Bach sacred music goes a long way, except around Easter when the *St. Matthew Passion* is the flavour of the month. Still, I believed Sean would jump at the opportunity to hear a prominent singer in the flesh of which, according to recent publicity shots, there was no shortage. (No dearth of girth, as Walter would have said.)

She who hesitates is saved; nevertheless, I returned Diana's call. At times I have to remind myself that Diana is not a woman to renew her ideas. She belongs to a generation that believes any ticket for a culturally elevating event must be used. Warm bodies must occupy seats purchased for *Swan Lake*, Beethoven's Ninth Symphony, *Rigoletto*, or *As You Like It*. Were the cultural hostage young, and by definition impressionable, so much the better. Exposure to the higher things should begin early. I have watched Diana work her way systematically through her telephone directory in order to unload two tickets to a recital of Bach's unaccompanied suites for cello, tickets I had refused.

Never having shared Diana's artistic compulsions — if you don't feel like going, stay home! — I figured I could probably use three tickets.

"But that's an odd number. It's difficult enough to unload a pair of tickets, but one is just about impossible. One always ends up with a stray widow. You must take four."

"Very well. I can probably fill three seats, and if it rains I'll have room for my coat."

"At the price I paid for those tickets that's very expensive checking. Do try to find a fourth. And you know you are all invited back here after the concert."

"I'll get cracking at it right away."

After promising to leave my four tickets with the doorman, Diana hung up. She still had two more seats to unload and the clock ticked relentlessly away.

၄

Sunday turned out to be the perfect day for a concert, heavy and humid with a promise of rain that did not materialize. The simple act of breathing required effort. It was the ideal afternoon to sit passively and be entertained.

Wearing my two piece black *tailleur*, never out of fashion because it was never in, I had accessorized with so much gold jewellery I felt like an Indian bride. To my right sat Sean, wearing a jacket and tie in deference to fifth row centre. Granted, the tie had been woven on a loom. Worn with a tattersall shirt, it evoked a time when people wove fabrics and threw pots and hammered silver in deadly earnest. Perhaps they still do, but I no longer know any.

To my left sat Craig, also wearing a jacket. He had drawn the line at a tie. Visible in the V of his open-necked shirt lay a heavy gold chain he seemed to wear all the time. To his left sat Jonathan in earth tones looking as though he had just stepped from a page in *Gentlemen's Quarterly*.

My first recruit had been Sean, whom I had telephoned shortly after speaking with Diana. Avoiding conventional preamble, I launched into my reason for the call: to wit, did he want to hear Francisco Bertolini on Sunday afternoon, followed by drinks chez Diana. He did. We agreed to meet at Place-Des-Arts twenty minutes before the recital was due to begin. During the slight flurry of preparations for meeting on Sunday afternoon the subject of Sean's moving in did not come up. I knew it must, sooner or later; but I would burn that bridge when the chickens were hatched.

Craig arrived back from New York on Saturday afternoon. By then the new bed had been delivered and made up. I had visited a local hardware store to purchase an unpainted table and straight-backed chair. Although spartan, the room was habitable. Craig looked dubious.

"I could stay across the hall with Jonathan. He invited me."

"I twisted arms to get that bed delivered on time, so the least you can do is sleep in it. And should you suspect I am laying a major guilt trip, you could well be right. Besides, I don't want to begin life in Queen's Court owing the neighbour favours."

Craig shrugged and proceeded to unpack while I told him about the recital.

"Who will be using the fourth ticket?" he asked.

"I don't know. Probably nobody."

"If you don't have anyone in mind could I ask Jonathan?"

"Do you want to?"

"Yes, it would be a way of saying thank you for putting me up."

I could think of no valid reason not to invite Jonathan, other than my innate reluctance to see any more of him than necessary. All of which explains how the four of us came to be seated in a row enveloped in that expectant hush which precedes the entrance of the artist.

Francisco Bertolini strode onstage to thunderous applause from the full house. Still handsome, in that glossy Italian way, he had the look of a man who never met a second helping he didn't like. But when he opened his mouth it was evident he had what it takes, namely a voice, large, focused, distinctive, with the special ping that separates a house tenor from an operatic star.

The recital began with a group of those Eighteenth-Century Italian songs over which voice students stumble and learn. If there was a unifying theme it turned on the pitfalls of love and ambition, temptations I appear to have outgrown. After applause and the customary walk offstage, Bertolini returned, basking in applause, to tackle Schubert. Most of the songs were familiar to me, even though my knowledge of German is scant. The trout was caught; the Erl-king killed the child; Death claimed the maiden. Fortunately the group ended with a cheery gondolier's song, even though the idea of a Venetian oarsman singing in German goes against nature.

Simple truths: there is no pasta I do not like; there are no songs by Fauré I do not like. Comfortable with a language I understood, I spun through the moonlight with the melancholy courtiers, sat on the riverbank with the lovers, and finished with a visit to the cemetery.

Much applause and several bows later we filed into the lobby for intermission. Craig and Jonathan sloped away, ostensibly to visit the men's washroom but more, I think, to avoid the other couples Diana had roped in to fill seats, earnest, middle-aged souls, the men in dark suits, the wives in frocks. They would have to be dealt with later at Diana's, but then we would be helped along by something from the bar.

"Shall we split a Perrier?" inquired Sean. "My treat."

"Love to."

We edged our way over to the bar, leaving Diana in charge of her group like a tour guide. As it was only mid-afternoon few of the audience felt inclined to drink. Sean filled one tall glass with Perrier; obviously we were going to share. What bothered me were not the germs (drinking from someone else's glass was forbidden by my mother), but the symbolism. If we shared a Perrier then must we share a life?

As if reading my thoughts, Sean, who had steered us behind a potted fern, took a swallow, then handed me the glass. "Have you had a chance to consider my proposition?"

Neither the place nor the time struck me as appropriate;

I was swept with a feeling of irritation bordering on anger. I handed back the glass without drinking.

"You mean about your moving in?"

"What else?"

"To tell you the truth, I've thought about it almost non-stop. I'm still weighing the pros and cons."

"And …?"

"I'm still ambivalent." I shrugged helplessly. "I'm so new at being a widow I'm not sure I don't need a breathing space."

Sean took a long, almost aggressive swallow of Perrier. Then, almost carefully, he smiled. "I certainly don't want to crowd you. Take all the time you need. Only remember; I have to start househunting pretty soon if you decide — well, that you prefer the status quo."

I smiled, a wan, defensive simile. Then, with a surge of relief, I spotted Craig and Jonathan heading our way. As they came closer I reached for the Perrier. Suddenly my throat felt cactus-dry, and it would be a while before I could dive into a scotch and water.

It was now time to head back into the auditorium for the second half of the program. I know I lack high seriousness, but I always enjoy the second half of a vocal recital more than the first. By now we have paid our dues to the German art song, permitting the singer to let down his guard and entertain. To my surprise he began with a group of American songs: Foster, Ives, Rorem; furthermore, because he approached the English language as a foreign tongue, he managed to make the words intelligible. English is not an easy language to sing, too many consonants; but Signor Bertolini approached our native tongue in the same way he had sung German. The result was idiomatic but intelligible diction. I gave him full marks.

Now came the part of the program we had all been anticipating, even those who sat rapt during the German songs. Francisco Bertolini had made his international reputation on the operatic stage. At this point he had fully warmed up his voice and was ready to turn himself loose on *Manon Lescaut*, *La Bohème*, and *Rigoletto*. The audience ate it up and rewarded the singer with the obligatory standing ovation. (One of Sean's more annoying traits is that he is always the first on his feet for a standing ovation.)

After a few bows, smiling, waving, and milking the audience for applause, the tenor returned to offer his signature tune as encore: "Nessun dorma" from *Turandot*. As the last notes rang out one could easily believe that no one would sleep in Peking, Shanghai, or even Vladivostok. Wisely, he scaled down the subsequent encores, moving from operetta through Tosti to "Be My Love."

It had been a generous program; it was also time to go home. A few die-hard enthusiasts kept applauding and shouting bravos, but the experience had wound down. Sated and satisfied, the audience filed out, ready for whatever the shank of the afternoon might have to offer. Diana herded us out of the auditorium, then divided us into groups for the taxi ride to her apartment. I was to go with Sean, Craig and Jonathan, three in the back seat of the cab, one in front with the driver. I think I might have figured that one out for myself, but Diana was on a roll.

In spite of the small number of our group, Diana's guests plus a few committee members and husbands, we arrived to find a bartender in black bow-tie, a maid in black uniform, and a white-coated woman in the kitchen presiding over the hors d'oeuvres. Both bartender and maid had the freshly scrubbed look of moonlighting college students. As we waited for drinks to be handed around on a silver tray, we all agreed it had been a wonderful recital, that he sang German very well for an Italian, that his forte was opera, no doubt about that, but that his French songs had been sung with great sensitivity. Yes, indeed.

A balding husband, who I suspected would have been far happier spending the afternoon playing golf, suggested crossly that Bertolini was carrying around quite a corporation, to which one of the committee wives chirpily observed that you don't get the same sound from an upright piano that you do from a concert grand. I was reminded of a gym teacher I once had in grade school who demanded, when I confessed to forgetting my running shoes, "What would happen if firemen forgot to answer fire alarms?" Too young to understand I had not been asked a question but given a mind fuck, I said nothing. Neither did the husband.

My scotch and water tasted on the far side of delicious, and I was on the point of paying my dues as guest and speaking to Diana's friends, when I witnessed a small episode. A non-smoker herself, Diana provides ashtrays for those who do. But nowadays where there's smoke there's ire. The balding husband, he who had made the observation about the singer's weight, lit a cigarette, moreover an American cigarette, far more aromatic than its bland Canadian counterpart. A woman, whose officious air identified her as his wife, stage whispered, "Ronald, you know what the doctor said about smoking!"

Ronald, to whom I had been introduced, but whose name I promptly forgot, inhaled right down to the tips of his tasselled loafers before replying. "The doctor didn't have to sit through two — hours of songs he did not understand."

I was amused to watch him pause before "hours of" while his mouth began to form "goddamn," but he reconsidered.

"You're the only one smoking." she hissed.

"There are ashtrays. And if you say one more goddamned word I'll smoke two simultaneously!"

At this point I eased myself away from the group. My sympathies lay with the husband, but I was unprepared to be spectator to a spat. I had my fill of being entertained. In a corner of the living room Sean was in deep discussion with a couple. The body language suggested high earnestness, beyond me at the moment; so I decided to visit the powder room, a.k.a. guest bathroom.

For some reason, to this day I don't know why, I decided to look in on the spare room where I had slept while Diana's guest. Perhaps I wanted to postpone my return to the party with its obligation to chat up the guests, but I moved towards my old room. Just inside the door, facing the bedroom, stood a large art deco chest of drawers. Bleached mahogany and topped by a semi-circular mirror etched with a border of parallel stripes, it brought to mind the Thirties, Syrie Maugham, and all-white rooms. Since the mirror faced the doorway a person standing in the passageway could see a reflection of the entire space. Craig and Jonathan stood talking and laughing, heads bent together almost conspiratorially. Suddenly Jonathan reached out and cradled Craig's cheek with a gesture so intensely intimate it caused me to inhale sharply. At that moment I understood the two men were lovers. Why else had Jonathan invited Craig to use his spare room. Why else had Craig been so lukewarm about my newly furnished spare room. Why else had Jonathan been roped into this afternoon's outing. Why else: shit!

My thinking was not nearly so linear as I was making it sound. A great deal of information had come crowding in on me, not least of which was the fact I now knew beyond all doubt that my son was gay. To be sure, I would have been naïve not to understand about Craig. But there is knowledge, and then there is knowledge. To realize, in a vague, unspecific, and completely imprecise way, that your son will probably never marry does not encompass the disquieting awareness that he is sleeping with your unsavoury neighbour.

Therein lay the core of the problem. I did not care one way or the other that Craig slept with men. What I did not know could not impinge. But suddenly, unexpectedly, unwillingly, I had been force fed a bite of the apple. I had been thrust into knowledge, and the experience turned out not to be liberating but infuriating. In fact, it took considerable self-restraint not to march into my former bedroom and bang their heads together.

Perhaps more wisely, I retraced my steps to the living room. Polishing off my drink in two swallows, I collared the young woman masquerading as maid and asked for another. Diana bustled up, fairly crackling with the hostess imperative.

"Louise, do go and talk to the McNallys. I know they make heavy weather, but they are all alone. They have a niece who lives in Victoria. Perhaps you might find common ground. I had to include them as she is tireless on the telephone. I am sure people buy tickets just so they can hang up, but there you are."

I was in no mood to be sociable, but it turned out I did not have to be. Mona McNally needed no more than a new pair of ears so she could expound at great length about nothing in particular. She delivered her platitudes like epigrams. "If more people went to concerts there would be less violence in the world." Her husband had, I suspect, been pummelled into submission years ago. He and I stood mute while his wife went on. She really hated to say, but what she hated to say took approximately ten minutes.

Rescue came in the form of Craig. Excusing himself he led me just out of earshot.

"Jonathan and I are off to a party. I've said goodbye and thank you to Aunt Diana. I don't know how late we will be, so I may bunk in with Jonathan — so as not to disturb you."

About to remark that the idea of his "bunking in" with the cretinous Jonathan bothered me far more than his coming late into the apartment, I reconsidered. A confrontation might or might not arise, but here and now was neither the appropriate place nor the telling time.

"Sure — whatever." I gave a shrug and turned away, but Craig had already begun to sidle towards the foyer lest he be trapped into saying goodbye to everyone in turn. By now several of the other guests had begun to peel away, either to dine out or return home for supper, slippers, and telly.

I too decided the time had come to leave. Diana had help to tidy up after the guests. Also my list of good deeds does not extend to helping hostesses muck out their houses after parties, no doubt a flaw in my character but one I have learned to accept. Uncharacteristically, Diana did not press me to stay; but then she must have had her fill of the concert, the guests, the duty drinks and finger foods.

I looked around for Sean. Since he had been my guest, in a manner of speaking, I could not very well flounce out without at least saying goodnight. Now that Craig was back in town I certainly did not want Sean staying over, Potiphar's wife and all that. Nor did I fancy bedding down in his austere and monastic apartment. What I wanted most of all was to go home, get out of my party clothes, and try to sort out what I had so unceremoniously discovered about my son.

"I'll be taking a cab back to Queen's Court," I volunteered. "Can I drop you on the way?"

"That would be very kind. Of course with Craig in town we must tread the stony path of virtue."

"We must."

We waited in the lobby while the doorman telephoned for a taxi. The McNallys scuttled past with a quick goodnight and a perfunctory wave, lest they feel obliged to offer us a lift. The taxi arrived, and we headed towards Sean's apartment, turning the ride into an isosceles triangle rather than a straight line. The taxi had begun life as a station wagon, meaning there was a fair bit of distance between passengers and driver. Perhaps this apparent isolation prompted Sean to reach for my hand.

"Your seem tense. Anything wrong?"

"No, nothing wrong. I am not tense, just very alert."

Sean laughed. "Sometimes it's difficult to differentiate." He paused to give my fingers a reassuring squeeze. "I really hate to push you, Louise, but my lease is up on the first of January. As you can well imagine, Christmas week is no time to move. That leaves me little room to get organized and out of my present digs. I really would like to move in with you;" he gave my unresponsive fingers another squeeze, "but I will have to sign a new lease pretty soon if — well — if it doesn't work out."

How could Sean have known what I had just learned about Craig, and how could he possibly have realized how unresponsive I felt towards his offer at this very moment. But I had been given a make or break opportunity to scuttle the issue once and for all.

"I can't do it, Sean. There's no point in beating around the bush. It is too soon after Walter's death for me to even consider another relationship. If it will make you feel any better, which it probably won't, I don't want Craig underfoot any longer than absolutely necessary. Maybe in a while — but that won't do you any good. Better to get cracking on finding a new place to live."

I paused. Sean withdrew his hand. "Convention demands I say I'm sorry. But I'm not going to be that dishonest. I'm neither sorry nor glad. I'm just not ready at the moment to undertake what you offer. What more can I say?"

Sean leaned forward to give the driver directions. We turned onto the street where Sean lived and drew up in front of his house.

"Thanks, Louise. I'm glad you levelled with me. I begin to househunt tomorrow."

"Whenever you feel like a home cooked meal, give me a call."

"Will do." He brushed my cheek with his lips and climbed out of the cab.

As I sat back for the drive to Queen's Court I realized Sean and I had just said goodbye for the second time. I doubted there would be a third.

Whatever misgivings I may have felt about shutting Sean out of my life were more than upstaged by those concerning Craig and Jonathan. Now that I knew, beyond all reasonable doubt, that something was going on between them, what was I to do with this knowledge? Had the man in question been someone I liked or, at the very least, a person who aroused no strong feelings one way or another, I would simply have gone with the flow. Having nothing to gain by suggesting I knew the score, I would have feigned a contented ignorance. Were the relationship to progress to the point where Craig wanted to talk, then I would be prepared to listen.

The problem, if such it could be called, arose from the reticence Craig and I had always shared about things personal. Every family copes in its own way. Were we to be guided by television we would, without a second's hesitation, blurt out everything from adultery to menstrual cramps. But privacy does not make for compelling drama. Craig and I talked at length about his work, my reading, our common acquaintances. We did not, however, discuss our personal lives.

If this is to be considered a fault, I must accept much of the blame. After Craig was born and I had shed my widow's weeds, I went out with a number of men. Craig visited his adoring grandmother, who displayed a tactful absence of curiosity about how I spent the evenings when she baby-sat. Craig grew up to understand that what Mother (I discouraged his calling me "Mummy") did on her time off was her own business. Then I met and married Walter Bingham, in all respects a stellar stepfather; but the pattern of reticence had been set.

Craig matured early and without fanfare; no cracking voice, pimples, mood swings, scenes, or brushes with the law. He experienced puberty in much the same way I went through menopause, without fuss or fanfare. Walter and Craig had a couple of "little talks," and I realized, not without a surge of relief, that my son was now mature enough to live as an autonomous being. Furthermore, Craig did not get sick smoking purloined cigarettes, wreck the car after too many beers, or get a girl pregnant.

Walter and I subscribed to our first answering service so we could eat dinner without calls for Craig, whose very reluctance to promote himself made him much sought after. Not to mention that he was extraordinarily handsome, black-haired and blue-eyed, with the body of a model for jockey shorts. More than just a hunk, Craig was also a dish. Small wonder the frankly middle-aged and no doubt somewhat jaded Jonathan found him attractive. What I failed to see, or even imagine, was what Craig saw in Jonathan. *De gustibus non disputandum est*, and sexual attraction can be as difficult to pin down as mist.

To be sure, Craig most probably did not know about Jonathan's business dealings. Possibly he did not mind being manipulated, especially when Jonathan "turned on the charm," to borrow an expression of my mother's. If there were only some way I could persuade Craig into seeing Jonathan as I did, then maybe the affair would wither on the vine. For me to confront Craig openly with my dislike and mistrust of his *inamorato* would precipitate a stand-off. Craig would conclude, wrongly, that I was edgy about his being gay, with the result that I was projecting all kinds of nebulous faults onto Jonathan. I would find myself cast in the role of outraged and intolerant parent.

If I wanted to break up this relationship, and I did, I must resort to guile and subterfuge. I did not have a plan; I did not like the idea of formulating a plan. For the first time, I intended to meddle in my son's life; and, specious though it may sound, I believed the end justified the means. No doubt Vlad the Impaler borrowed the same argument; but I took comfort from knowing I did not want Jonathan impaled, only exiled.

I did not yet have a plan; but, as the saying goes, "Necessity is the mother of invention." Shameful though the admission may be, I find that clichés reassure. There is a continuity to banality, and drifting into an affair with your mother's new neighbour is about as banal as it gets.

I sent out for pizza with all the trimmings. My discovery

at Diana's stunned appetite, and I wanted comfort food: hot, soft, chewy, and rich.

When I awoke the next morning I found the lights I had left on for Craig still burned. I did not have to look into his bedroom to know he had slept at Jonathan's, as I had been certain he would. But leaving a light burning in the home, in case my boy should return late, satisfied some sort of deeply atavistic, not to mention masochistic, maternal urge. It also strengthened my resolve to take arms against a sea of troubles. If borrowing Shakespeare has become a cliché, then at the very least it has the merit of being triple-A, twenty-four carat, vintage, executive class, and suitable for framing.

7

$\mathcal{O}$nly slightly overwrought by more coffee than I usually drink in the morning, I found my mind shifting into over-drive. I could not openly attack Jonathan; he had given me no cause. A gut feeling does not provide a firm foundation for a case, and Craig would spring to his defense. Were I to find a chink in the armour, something that would discredit him in Craig's estimation, then I might prevail. But how was I to discover that chink? How indeed?

Coffee makes me want to pee. On my way back through my bedroom I glanced at a pair of antique decanters which I had left on the windowsill until such time as I had a proper place to display them. A handsome set, they had been given to Walter as a wedding present for his first marriage. Of early-American clear glass, now flecked with the spots of age, the four sides of each decanter sloped inwards from a square base, making them appear almost like truncated obelisks. The feature that particularly amused me was a tiny flange that hinged upwards from the neck to fit neatly over a metal loop attached to the stopper so that a tiny padlock could prevent servants or loiterers from taking a nip. For a household that had always bought scotch, gin, and vodka in the largest available size, the idea of locking up the cherry brandy or the ratafia delighted me.

Suddenly, like Good Deed Dottie in the comic strip of my youth, I saw a lightbulb flash on in the balloon above my head. I would offer the decanters to Jonathan on consignment, then arrange for someone to buy them. At the last moment I would shamelessly invoke the woman's prerogative of wanting to change her mind, and reclaim the decanters. What I hoped to learn was whether the markup, which I am certain Jonathan took on these transactions, remained within the bounds of reason or edged towards the larcenous. In other words, was he an honest dealer or a rip-off artist?

It was a gamble. He might manage to sell the pair to a regular client before my shill had a chance to make an offer. I was very attached to the decanters, moreso because they had belonged to Walter. Yet Walter had been so intimate a part of my life that I did not need decanters, or photographs, or my wedding ring to keep memory green. I had loved him, and that love would be a part of me until my death.

Ideas breed ideas. Were Jonathan to accept the decanters

on consignment, I would have proof positive he was dealing out of his apartment in defiance of the co-op by-laws. I could then raise the issue at the next annual meeting and question why this contravention of rules was being overlooked. I could not be the only resident of Queen's Court who was *au courant* about Jonathan's operation. Yet challenging him before the board of directors would not help my present problem; namely, how to drive a wedge between him and Craig. Whatever the outcome of my scheme, the first step was to find myself a collaborator.

Whomever I chose must be someone Jonathan did not know, also someone he could not readily link with me. The person in question must be plausible; Jonathan was no fool. My accomplice must deal easily with money; this was no nickel-and-dime operation. Suddenly the synapses, goosed by an overdose of caffeine, flashed a name onto my mindscreen. Who else but my former sister-in-law, Helen Morrison. Rich and verging on eccentric, she would be just the kind of customer who might be interested in early-American glass, or art deco, or Eighteenth-Century French china for that matter.

As I sat, pondering how best to enlist Helen in my enterprise, I decided to tell her the truth: that my son was involved with an unsuitable man, and I wanted to get him uninvolved. I had a scheme for a scam; I needed an accomplice, someone smart and plausible, and she fitted the job description. The payoff would be lunch or dinner at a restaurant of her choice plus a stack of chips to be cashed in when she needed a favour in return.

A surge of energy propelled my to the telephone, only to be met with an answering tape. Helen's unmistakable rasp delivered a message. "Due to the current condition of the Dow Jones average I am unable to come to the telephone. Leave a message and a number. If the bulls banish the bears I may return your call." Since mine was not a subject to be committed to tape, I hung up, just as Craig let himself into the apartment.

"Top of the morning, Mater!" he began with false heartiness. "As you can see, we got in late, and I didn't want to wake you."

"That's very considerate of you, Craig; but I wouldn't have minded. One of the hostages to advancing age is unbroken sleep. Hearing you come in would not have been a problem. Would you like some breakfast?"

"I had coffee and toast with Jonathan. We're going out for brunch, then I'm taking the afternoon train to Ottawa."

"Isn't this rather sudden?"

"Not really. My Vancouver dealer has decided to open a branch gallery in Ottawa, and I want to check it out. I'll just be overnight."

"Where will you stay?"

"Jonathan has a friend who lives in Ottawa, Roger Clarke. He has a guest room I can use."

"I met him when he was down visiting Jonathan. I liked him. He seems like a very civilized man."

"That's good to hear. I'll be taking him out to dinner, as a good guest ought." Craig moved towards the guestroom. "I'll take a shower and toss a few things into an overnight bag."

"Will I expect you for dinner tomorrow evening?"

"Why don't I give you a call. I may be going to an opening with Jonathan. It all depends on when I get back."

"Fair enough." I watched Craig go into his room and close the door. My coffee high was beginning to wear off; and I felt just a little dejected, almost as if I had been jilted. Perhaps "jilted" was not the right word, but I still felt very seriously upstaged. I had really looked forward to Craig's visit, to have him stay in my new apartment and see how well I was managing on my own. I had hoped for a couple of days of just hanging out, as the young say: a little lunch, a spot of gallery going, perhaps a bit of shopping, maybe tea at the Ritz. Foolish, fun, holiday treats. Instead I found myself sitting glumly on the sidelines watching my son drift into an affair with a man I did not like.

Not to mention Sean. Now you see him; now you don't. In spite of vigilant security and a formidable doorman I felt as though my new apartment had a revolving door. Men spun in and out. Never mind. I was not going gently into that goddamned good night, and as soon as Craig got himself off to Ottawa I intended to track down Helen and put my plan into action.

Strike while the irony is hot. I telephoned Helen two more times before the real voice replied. "Hello?"

"Helen, it's Louise. I want to involve you in a scam."

"Thank God for that. For a terrified moment I though you might want me to play bridge or sell raffle tickets."

"On both counts you are safe. However, I need a partner in crime. My son is getting himself involved with a highly unsuitable man, and I want you to help me prove he is dishonest."

"Before we go any further I have to ask you one question: Are you a closet homophobe, or do you really think this guy is bad news?"

"Believe me, Helen, I've gone over that question many times, in the privacy of my closet. It's not that Craig is seeing a man: I'm certain this person is neither the first nor the last. But this one is most definitely not son-in-law material."

"But he is — pardon the expression — suitable for framing."

"In a manner of speaking. As well as leading my son down the garden path, I suspect he is operating a business out of his apartment in contravention of the building by-laws. He must have something on someone on the board of directors. And even if Craig were not involved, this man gets up my nose."

"Will what you want me to do send me to jail for ten years?"

"Not even ten days. What I want is for you to pretend you are a collector of early-American glass. I plan to let him have a pair of decanters on consignment, and I want you to show interest. Then I can compare the estimated price with what he wants you to pay. I strongly suspect he is not on the up and up. Furthermore, I have a strong, not to say overpowering suspicion, that he took advantage of the woman who formerly owned this apartment."

Then, after Helen had brought her cigarettes and ashtray to the phone, I told her about my initial meeting with Jonathan; the telephone calls from the niece, Beatrice Lane; my finding the journal which I read, and my doubts about the French china and silver tankard. Helen listened without interruption, which told me she was interested.

"On balance, he sounds like a nasty piece of work," she observed. "What specifically do you want me to do?"

While Helen puffed audibly into the receiver we worked out a plan. Once I had consigned the decanters to Jonathan, I would alert Helen. She would then get in touch with him, claiming he had been recommended by someone met at a party; she couldn't remember the person's name. Having gone to Jonathan's apartment she would express interest in my decanters, then insist she wanted to consider the purchase. Once home, she would telephone and we would compare our respective prices. After a while she would inform Jonathan she had decided not to purchase the decanters, then I would say I had changed my mind about selling them.

The plan seemed perfectly straight forward, and I promised to call as soon as I had worked out my deal with Jonathan.

"Should I turn up for the viewing heavily veiled, my eyes ringed with kohl?"

"Nothing too cloak-and-dagger. Perhaps even dowdy. You know how women who collect unusual and expensive items never buy clothes, unless from thrift shops or the Salvation Army. Be earnest rather than clever. That way he can take advantage of you more easily."

Helen laughed down the line. "Are you sure you haven't been working for the CIA? You're pretty devious for a recently widowed housewife."

"I want to win this one. No holds barred. I'll let you know when Jonathan has the decanters."

As luck would have it, I had barely put down the receiver when the doorbell gave its sharp jangle. I opened to find Jonathan holding a liquor store bag. He did not smile, and even in the muted light of the passageway he looked the worse for wear.

"I'm returning a few things Craig left in my guest room. Now that you have furnished yours, I presume he will be sleeping here."

"Thanks for giving him a roof," I said, trying to sound as though I meant what I said. "By the way, will you come in for a moment? I have something I want to show you."

Jonathan entered my apartment as though he owned a controlling interest. Unable to find a suitable surface on which to put down the plastic bag, he handed it to me. I set it on the kitchen counter before pointing out the decanters.

"I'm thinking of selling them," I said casually, but observing Jonathan's reaction closely. "Would they be of any interest to you?"

He picked up one of the pair as if it were a piece of pressed glass from a dollar store. "American. Pity about the marks in the glass." Turning the piece in a slow, appraising manner he pushed his lips together, like a politician on TV who has just delivered a sound byte. "I suppose I might get two hundred or so for the pair."

"What is your commission?"

"On anything under five hundred dollars I take twenty-five percent."

I almost had to bite my tongue not to ask how he had managed to bend the co-op rule about running a business in the building, but that would all come out in the wash. "Sounds fair enough," I said non-committally. "Do you want to take them along? They aren't really my style, and with a flat to furnish, every bit helps."

"Doesn't it though. Well, I'll be running along." Jonathan picked up the decanters and moved towards the door. In the more uncompromising light of my living room he looked like someone who had been out on a weekend tear. Had Craig given him a real workout? If so, he took after his father. Of course I too had been younger then and raring to go. I could almost have felt sorry for Jonathan. The price of whoopee is a crosshatching of tiny, unflattering wrinkles. I could have felt sorry, but not sorry enough not to pick up the telephone and inform Helen the decanters were now waiting to be traded.

My nefarious scheme must have captured Helen's imagination, as I subsequently learned she wasted little time in calling Jonathan. Her voice over the telephone — deep, articulate, rough around the edges — must have suggested a wealthy eccentric, as only three days later she was taking the fragrant elevator up to his apartment.

The period that elapsed between my consigning the decanters to Jonathan and the subsequent telephone call from Helen turned out to be without dimension, as though time itself had ceased to flow and folded in upon itself, like a telescope. Diana telephoned, and in a quiet, low-keyed, and quite un-Diana-like tone of voice told me she had something to discuss and would I come for lunch. The invitation was just that, an invitation, not an edict; and its very understatement obliged me to accept.

Over lasagne and salad she informed me matter-of-factly, as though she were discussing the weather, that she had been diagnosed with uterine cancer and was going into hospital for surgery in six days. The frozen lasagne was not very good. Perhaps just as well, as I suddenly lost my desire to eat.

"When did you learn?" I asked, putting down my fork.

"This morning."

"You never mentioned anything to me!" I snapped, trying unsuccessfully to keep accusation out of my voice.

"I saw no need to alarm you until I was certain. And so far

you are the only one who knows. I must insist you keep the news to yourself. I dread the thought of being discussed over bridge."

"Have you told the children?"

"Not yet, but I will." Diana paused for a small bite of her lunch. "I wanted you to be the first to know. You have known me longer than anyone else in my life."

"You've really taken the wind out of my sails, Diana. For once I don't know what to say."

"What is there to say. It is unfortunate, but it must be dealt with."

"How long have you suspected — you had a problem?" I fumbled for words, more precisely for synonyms. In spite of all the years I had known Diana, I could not employ the clinically precise terms: fibroids in the uterus, vaginal bleeding, cervical cancer. She was probably the last living throwback to a generation that spoke in hushed tones of bodily functions. They spoke of "down there," "the curse," and "the change of life." They carried book matches in their handbags, not to light cigarettes but to strike over the toilet after they had "spent a penny." This was no time to brandish the dictionary. I must tread softly.

"For a few weeks now. I have had — symptoms. When they persisted I thought I had better call the doctor. She ordered some tests, and I learned the results in her office this morning."

I realized that no details or hard information were to be

forthcoming. Nor did I press for them. These were Diana's cards, and she must play them as she saw fit. I also understood, knowing Diana, that she had not made a bid for sympathy. Rather, she had information to impart. I reacted in the best way I knew, namely to avoid fuss and seek solutions.

"Would you like me to come and stay here when you get out of the hospital?"

"That's very kind of you, Louise, but I have arranged for nurses for as long as I may need them. What you could do is just keep an eye on things. You know: make sure there is food in the fridge, liquor in the bar. I'll open a housekeeping account so you won't be out of pocket. I'm sure to have visitors." She paused. "It might be more convenient for you to move into the building. I decided to buy that vacant apartment I wanted you to look at. In this building it will only appreciate in value. I bought the place furnished. Of course the previous owner took personal items and a few bits of family furniture, but the place is essentially habitable. I make the suggestion only because it might be less bother for you than shuttling back and forth between our two buildings. Can I pop your lunch into the microwave?"

"No thanks, Diana. I'm just not very hungry."

"As I was saying, you could move into the empty flat, just until I am back on my feet. I don't plan to do anything about it until I have recovered. Then I may sublet, at least until the place has appreciated enough to make selling it worthwhile."

"Let me think about it, Diana. I'll do whatever is best for us both."

Even as I spoke I knew I was being manipulated. Diana was determined to get me into Three Forest Road, and cancer was as good a lever as any. I know I should have been ashamed of myself for being such a sourball, just as I understood that in the battle for supremacy we use the weapons at hand.

At the same time I could not ignore Diana's observation that I had known her longer than anyone else. She was right. We had grown up together. I still have the strand of pearls she gave me when I graduated from high school, one year after her. I had been her bridesmaid, in dusty-pink taffeta and the pearl necklace. In turn she had been my matron of honour in champagne chiffon in which she had never looked more beautiful. She hired a nanny to look after her young children and spent days with me after Serge was killed. I was godmother to her children, rather a slapdash one I am the first to admit. She was my attendant when I married Walter Bingham. She balked at wearing chiffon again and suggested something with polkadots. I have always believed in permitting citizen's arrest for anyone wearing polkadots; we compromised on a tailored silk suit in pale lavender. The gardenias she carried had been so bashed about that when she came down the aisle their petals were turning brown, but nobody appeared to notice. Whenever I flew to Montreal for a visit I stayed with her on Mayfair Crescent. Flu prevented her from coming out to Victoria when Walter died, but she telephoned me every day for three weeks.

Diana and I were woven into the very fabric of one another's lives. Yet much as I wanted to put my arms around her, to tell her I loved her and that we would work out everything together, I understood that doing so would punch holes in the structure she had erected around herself to deal with this crisis. Raw emotion was the enemy, even more than the invasive illness. And were I to indulge myself in a naked display of feeling, would I be doing so to shore up Diana or to unburden myself of pent-up stress and a possible feeling of guilt for being so hale and hearty? I could not be sure, so I toyed with my salad and merely said, "I will do whatever you think best. If you would prefer me to move into the apartment downstairs, then I shall do so."

"Thanks. I knew I could count on you. Would you prefer coffee or tea?"

"What are you having?"

"I prefer tea at noon."

"That will suit me nicely."

"By the way, Louise, considering my schedule for the next few weeks, I have resigned as chairman of the St. Luke's Christmas bazaar. They will have to find their own volunteers, so you are off the hook."

I laughed theatrically. "Now I will have to shop for your

Christmas present in earnest. I had counted on finding a suitable attic treasure to put under the tree."

"A bottle of sherry will do nicely. I have a feeling I'm going to need it." With that Diana got up to plug in the kettle.

✧

THE NEWS ABOUT Diana pushed my other concerns far from the centre of my consciousness. How trivial and unimportant now seemed Jonathan's business ethics, particularly regarding his purchase and sale of things nobody needed. Decanters, china, silver, what were these but marginal and unnecessary adjuncts to anyone's life. Diana was ill, perhaps gravely so. She could recover, go into remission, or die. And even if she recovered she still had to face the terrifying C-word with all its implications. Compared to that major hurdle, whether or not Craig was sleeping with the neighbour did not much matter on the cosmic scale.

Back in my apartment, I took a shower, although I was not dirty and too much washing dries my skin. But I needed the therapy of soothing hot water. When I emerged from the bathroom, semi-scalded but marginally more cheerful, I noticed the message light flickering on my telephone. The call came from Ottawa: Craig's voice told me he intended to stay two or three more days in the nation's capital and that he would let me know when he would be returning.

Although I was now preoccupied with Diana, forces had

been set in motion. As I was to learn from a message on my answering machine a couple of days later. Helen had been to visit Jonathan and wanted me to telephone for a report. At least her tale would take my mind off other concerns. I dialled, and Helen answered after four rings.

"Helen, it's me; sorry, it is I, Louise. I have to hand it to you. No grass grows under your feet. You went to visit my neighbour?"

"Did I not. I wore a crocheted sweater, rubber-soled shoes, and diamonds, looking every inch the dotty dame who would be interested in early glass and the like. Also, you're right about the man. Charming and alarming — a very grand fairy. I almost thought I should kneel and kiss the ring. Anyway, to cut to the chase, he wants five hundred bucks for the pair of decanters. I said I'd think it over."

"Interesting. He told me he expected to get around two hundred. Now I'll get in touch with him and say I've changed my mind. I can't thank you enough."

"No problemo. I wouldn't have missed visiting his lair for anything. Talk about Period Brothel. I haven't seen so many swags, tassels, gilt frames, and pedestals since my trip to St. Petersburg. Oh, and by the way, I asked about the china, the plates with the pink border. He wants a price that's off the charts — thousands. I asked how he acquired the set, and he claims it was a gift from a little old lady to whom he had been kind. She had also given him the tankard. It was quite a tale. Rolaids not included. The problem is that if he is challenged about the acquisition, it will be his word against that of the niece."

"You're right. Possession does give presumption of owner-ship. Anyhow, thanks again. Let me know when you'd like to have lunch."

Mindful of Diana's injunction, I hung up without mentioning my cousin's illness. The temptation to unburden myself, to tell the tale and through the telling to lighten the load on my spirit, was almost overwhelming. But I denied myself the luxury of confession. Instead I telephoned Jonathan and found him at home.

"Jonathan," I began, making my voice just a little bit breathy, "I hope you won't be cross with me — but I've changed my mind about selling the decanters. Please don't be angry."

"Not in the least," he replied with ill-concealed irritation. "Believe it or not, I think I have a buyer."

"You do? What is she — or he prepared to pay?"

"What I told you. Two hundred for the pair. That is, should she decide to buy."

"I hope you won't disapprove of my invoking my woman's privilege of changing her mind," (How I hated admitting to that stale, antebellum, feminine stupidity.) "but I realized Craig would be very sorry to see them go. He was very close to his stepfather, and I know he would like to have them. It's more for him than for me."

Jonathan laughed, suggesting a truce. I had him, the bastard. "In that case," he began, almost affably, "Of course you shall have them back." He paused for a moment. "By the way, has Craig returned from Ottawa?"

"Not yet, but I expect him tomorrow afternoon."

"As long as you are home, why don't I bring the decanters over."

"That would be very kind."

A few moments later, the doorbell rang. An unsmiling Jonathan thrust the decanters at me.

"Thank you," I said without embellishment.

He turned away, paused, then veered around to face me again. This time the smile was in place. "When Craig gets in, would you ask him to call me?"

"Of course." I closed the door feeling not unlike an Elizabethan bawd or go-between. I would have been more amused had the client not been my son. But — what the hell — I had my decanters back and the goods on Jonathan. How many other clients had he bilked? A hypothetical question, but one that did little to sweeten my disposition.

I telephoned Diana and asked if she would like me to swing by with the makings of dinner. She accepted gladly, claiming she wanted to clear her desk before entering the hospital. Diana is nothing if not organized, her desk a paradigm of neatness. What she really needed was not to be alone, and my offer to make dinner gave me a legitimate reason to come over. The last thing in the world she wanted or needed was the kind of moist, hand-wringing sympathy that turns the invalid into an object of pity. Nobody wants to be reduced to the status of object. Perhaps Diana would not have thought of herself in quite that way, but she was shrewd enough to understand the uncompromising condescension that goes with being felt sorry for. Pity is a demeaning attitude, unlike compassion. The problem arises from trying to tell them apart. On a moving arm, how does one distinguish a real Rolex from one bought in the street?

It is difficult to go far wrong with kidney lamb chops. With pilaff and salad they add up to a feast, and the meal is one I can make blindfolded. As I slid the chops into the oven, Diana poured herself a stiff gin and tonic instead of her customary sherry. I fortified myself with a scotch and joined Diana at the kitchen table.

"Louise," she began without preamble, "I want to ask you a favour."

"Is it illegal, immoral, or fattening?"

"None of the above. I am seeing the notary tomorrow; I want to revise my will, and he suggested drawing up a new document rather than adding codicils."

"I understand a new will is more foolproof. Walter always said so."

"Precisely. Needless to say the children are my principal beneficiaries. Christine is a lawyer; she will be my principal executor, along with the notary himself. But I would like a third executor, one who understands the situation and who won't be swayed by favouritism. I am fully aware you find all my children equally tiresome — not without cause I am the first to admit; but they are my offspring. Would you be willing to be the third executor?"

"Slow down a minute, Diana. You sound as though the Grim Reaper is heading over here on a motorcycle. I should be astonished if you don't make a full recovery."

"That is not the point. Sooner or later I will be called, as tedious Aunt Phoebe used to say; and, surgery or no, I want to leave my affairs in order."

On the pretext of turning down the oven, I poured myself another scotch. Talk of wills always makes me want to howl or giggle, often both at once. "Diana," I began as I sat, "I hate to ask, but am I a beneficiary? I only ask because, if I am, won't I be in a conflict of interest?"

Diana took a swallow of her drink and set down the glass deliberately. "You are a beneficiary. Of course you are a beneficiary. But you also have more than your share of that uncommon commodity known as common sense. You will be fair. And let me hasten to assure you that the will will be — can I say that? — as airtight as legally possible. But there is always something unaccounted for, the contents of the apartment, for instance. Even if I leave written instructions, there can still be disagreements; people can become very strange when it comes to dividing up the spoils. Who gets the silver? Who gets the Tom Thompson? Who gets the Baccarat sconces? In spite of their good jobs, the children all live like squatters. Maybe the sconces should be sold and the funds divided. The children will listen to you, and to the notary. You have gravitas. Will you do it?" Diana giggled into her now empty glass. "The last request of a dying woman?"

"If you like. I have silver of my own. I don't much like the Thompson. And Baccarat sconces do not sit well on IKEA. So, yes, I'll be one of the executors. That is if you don't outlive me."

Diana stood. "Do I have time for a dividend?"

"Always."

She went to the counter to pour another gin. "You are sure to outlive me, Louise. Only the good die young, and you are not good. Nor are you bad. You tread the moral middle ground: nature plus nurture plus expediency."

I burst out laughing. "Thank you for your vote of confidence. I think I'll start the pilaff."

"You mustn't take offence." Diana took a lethal swallow of gin. "I suppose what I mean to say is that you are neither sanctimonious nor sordid. When the time comes to make decisions, you will make the right ones."

"As long as the notary is coming tomorrow, could we get that in writing?"

"It won't be necessary. I am trying to pay you a compliment without sounding fulsome. Now, if you haven't already made salad, don't bother — unless you want some yourself. I ate an orange this morning and an apple this afternoon. It won't keep the doctor away, but I think I have had sufficient fibre for one day. And there is an ice cream cake in the freezer. I intend to indulge myself until the *Dies Irae*. Shall we have a little red wine with our lamb?"

Not surprisingly the gin and red wine, not to mention stress, left Diana comatose. Shortly after we had eaten, she excused herself to go to bed. After tidying up the kitchen and turning off the lights I was on the point of leaving when, struck by an idea, I went to check the silver bowl on the small, marble-topped table beside the front door, where Diana kept her keys. Sure enough, the keys to number 508, the number printed neatly on a plastic tag, hung from a ring attached to a pewter thistle. For a supposedly French city, Montreal has more than its share of Scottish fallout.

I had been guilty of a fib when I told Diana I looked at the vacant apartment in this building while househunting. Now that she was suggesting I move in for a while, I decided to sneak a look. Taking the elevator, which smelled of pine air freshener, I let myself into 508 and groped for the light switch. Although smaller than Diana's apartment, number 508 was well laid out. A large living room faced the mountain. To the right a generous alcove could be closed off by sliding doors. Another L-shaped space adjacent to the kitchen held a dining table. Down a short passageway past ample closets lay the master bedroom and a recently refurbished bathroom. The apartment had been furnished with a kind of studied neutrality. Corners had not been cut; everything looked well constructed and substantial, but the plain lines, sepia fabrics, grey walls, and beige curtains made the place feel like a boardroom or a first-class airline departure lounge.

All personal touches had been removed, but someone had left a book of paper matches on the glass coffee table. The crimson cover positively glowed against the monochromatic surroundings. Staying here for a while would be no hardship. I might even buy a potted plant for colour and company. Turning off the lights, I went upstairs to Diana's to return the key. No light seeped under her bedroom door. I was pleased she was able to sleep.

I took a taxi back to Queen's Court. Just as I was paying the driver, Jonathan walked up. "We must both have been out for dinner," he offered as opener.

"Just visiting my cousin." As we entered the building I said good evening to the night doorman. Jonathan gave a curt nod. We walked down the hall to the elevator. I pushed the button. After a moment we heard a distant clank.

"This damn thing takes forever!" Jonathan pushed the button three times to no avail. I wondered whether I, too, would turn into a compulsive button pusher after a few months in the building. We stood waiting.

"Did Craig get back from beautiful downtown Ottawa?"

"Not yet. He left a message on my voicemail saying he planned to stay a couple more days."

"He did?" The question sounded almost like an accusation.

"He said he'd let me know. Shall I let you know in turn?"

"No, don't bother. He'll give me a call."

The elevator arrived. As we rode in silence to our floor, I had a distinct feeling that Jonathan was put out. Body language does not lie. At our floor the door creaked open. Jonathan held out his arm, indicating I was to get off first; and after saying perfunctory goodnights we went into our respective apartments.

∽

The following morning Craig called to say he would be arriving in Montreal this afternoon and that Roger Clarke was coming with him. Roger would stay in Jonathan's guest-room, meaning Craig would stay with me. As I put down the receiver, I wondered briefly where Craig would have slept had Roger not decided to visit, a not very productive kind of speculation, and I turned my mind to other things.

When Diana's daughter Christine gave birth to twins, about eight years ago, she carried on as though she had just invented motherhood. First children are a milestone in any life, more so when the ultrasound comes up with a double. Most women manage to have the baby and continue to parti-cipate in the human race. Not Christine. She flung herself into motherhood with the zeal of a flagellant and managed to alienate almost everyone, including her mother. We have all raised children of our own; and, miraculously, they survived toys that were not consumer-approved, they walked to school without being molested, and they endured the occasional slap without going into therapy. What we minded most was being lectured by Christine. Not content with being a model mother, she felt obliged to broadcast her theories, as if pleading a case before a silent but hostile court.

I was in Victoria when Christine had her conversion. On the Road to Damascus she met a nanny, with the result that peace and order entered her life. She resigned the children to a no-nonsense English girl, engaged to a medical student, and went back to practising law. She stopped being a bore and rejoined the Earth People.

She was floored by the news that her mother had cancer and took time off to fly in just before Diana was to go in for surgery. Christine intended to take Diana to the hospital and see her settled. My responsibility would begin when Diana was well enough to return to her apartment, at which point I would move to 508 for as long as necessary.

Christine's arrival meant I would have time to spend with Craig, providing he had time to spend with me. It also occurred to me that I had better pay a visit to the market as, like that of Mother Hubbard, my cupboard was bare.

I was glad not to have planned an elaborate meal, as Craig announced that he was taking us all out to dinner, namely Jonathan, Roger, and me. Nothing too grand; Roger knew of a good Italian restaurant that didn't charge an arm and a leg. For just a moment I thought of digging in my heels and either begging off or suggesting that I would like to have a meal alone with my son. But Diana's illness had taken the starch out of my sails, and I decided to follow the current instead.

"I picked up some scotch and gin on my way from the station," said Craig after he had put his bag away in the spare room, "so I asked them to come by first for a drink."

"What time? I have to paint my face and tame my hair."

"Not at all. You look fine just as you are."

I was sorely tempted to observe that when one goes out with a mean queen like Jonathan, one leaves nothing to chance. "I would like to change. It's not often I am taken out to dinner by my son and heir."

If there was asperity in my tone, Craig appeared not to notice, and I went into my bathroom. Careful makeup is the contemporary equivalent of a helmet and visor, protection in the lists, be they merely social. My dark dress with jacket, medium heeled pumps, and plenty of gold jewellery stood in for chain mail and a shield, and instead of wielding a broadsword I carried a big dose of attitude.

8

When I am shuffling around the retirement home with the aid of a walker, I will look back on this particular evening as a milestone or Rubicon, a movement forward allowing for no retreat. By the time Roger and Jonathan rang the bell and invaded my apartment, I realized they had already imbibed that indeterminate quantity known as a "couple of drinks." Not that they staggered and slurred their words, but there was about them an aura of expansion, a heightened geniality that carried all before it.

"Darling, how elegant you look!" was Jonathan's opening salvo. To be sure, the last time we had drinks together I wore jeans, but the greeting still verged on overkill. Roger only kissed me on both cheeks, Montreal fashion, and announced he was pleased to see me again.

"Won't you pass through," I said, borrowing a greeting from Masterpiece Theatre, but Jonathan had already made a direct line for the one comfortable chair. While Craig improvised martinis, using an empty mason jar and a kitchen fork, I placed a block of reasonably good cheddar on a plate with some crackers. A little food might help to absorb the liquor, although both men were so diet conscious they would probably refuse my downmarket hors d'oeuvres.

As Craig handed me a scotch and water I turned towards Roger, who was, like me, perched on a straight-backed chair. I could not help wondering why we were not having our drinks in Jonathan's apartment, where we could have all sat in comfortable chairs. However, the guests had been invited to my apartment; and, by virtue of being the only woman present, I had become hostess by default.

"What brings you to Montreal again so soon?" I asked. "We are all delighted to see you — *ça va sans dire* — but shouldn't you be minding the store?"

"I have an assistant on call, so I came down to finish a little business and to tie off a few loose ends from my last visit. And there's an exhibition at the museum I want to see. Actually I come down quite often, to Jonathan's lasting dismay."

"I barely had time to change the sheets," interjected Jonathan. "Ordinarily my cleaning woman makes up the beds, but she is off this week. And Craig has been using the room."

There was a brief pause, then Roger smiled. "I didn't know Craig had been staying with you."

Jonathan leaned forward to take a cracker from the plate. As he did so, Roger winked at Craig, who gave a half smile. For just a moment I doubted my eyes. Had I really seen what I thought I saw? Were Roger and Craig …? No. Not possible. But that brief moment had shimmered with intimacy. Sex hovered in the air like a wisp of smoke from a Turkish cigarette. I know it says in the Rule Book for Mothers that we are supposed to cut our children some slack; but, if my suspicions turned out to be correct, then Craig's idea of fidelity was not being in bed with two people at the same time.

It was becoming all too evident that I knew very little about my son. Yet why should I be surprised? We had not shared a common roof, except for visits, since he was a teenager. Walter and I had retired to Victoria; Craig lived in Vancouver, same province but different cities. Furthermore, ours had been a household that valued privacy. Walter and I imposed minimal restrictions, preferring to teach by example rather than fiat. When Craig finally moved out from under the parental roof, I watched him go with equal parts regret and relief. I did not encourage him to bring his laundry home.

It is hardly original to observe that we put on different faces or masks for different people. When Craig came to spend weekends in Victoria I knew without having to be told that his accounts of what he had been doing underwent some careful editing. I did not wish it otherwise. Unlike characters on American television drama, who are always lobbying for complete disclosure, I firmly believe we all have parts of our lives that should remain private. Too much truth is like too much sunlight; they both cause cancer.

Suddenly I was learning things about Craig that I would have preferred to have ignored. Were he to be "on" with Roger, well and good. I liked Roger; Craig could do a lot worse. But the relationship with Jonathan, were there indeed such a relationship, had me puzzled, more than puzzled, provoked. However I had nothing to go on but suspicions; and, when in doubt, do nothing.

The conversation flowed around me as though I were perched on a rock in a river. Craig also said little. I have noticed that those who spend their time making something out of nothing — be it painting, music, or print — do not feel obliged to engage in small talk. Besides, with Jonathan and Roger performing their conversational high-wire act, Craig and I paid our dues as audience.

"I heard a wonderful parable the other day," began Jonathan, "from one of my clients. It seems a rich man was in love with three women — My God! Can you imagine! — anyway, that's the story. He didn't know which one he wanted to marry, so a wise old uncle — is there such a creature as a wise old uncle? Mine was a complete idiot. But to the point, this wise old uncle suggested the young man give each of the three women five thousand dollars to do with as she wished. How they spent the money would give him an idea of which one he should marry." Jonathan finished his drink. "I don't suppose I could have another of these?" He handed his glass to Craig. "Can you hear me out there in the kitchen?"

"Sure can," replied Craig.

"Well, the man in the story gave each of his ladies five thousand. At the end of a week he checked in to learn how each had spent the money. It seems the first had spent hers on making herself more beautiful. She became a blond, took Botox injections, acquired acrylic fingernails, and bought clothes: a wired bra, platform stiletto pumps, leather mini, which she wore with a Peter Pan blouse, combining the nice and the naughty." Jonathan reached for another cracker. "The second woman spent her money on gifts for the man: a DVD player, golf clubs, Cuban cigars, and a gold signet ring. The third, with an eye to their future, invested the money at ten per cent. Which one did he marry?"

We all murmured a disclaimer.

"The one with the big tits!"

We all laughed on cue. Whether or not we found the joke amusing, we rose to the social stimulus and mimed amusement. I have never been convulsed by big-tit jokes. My own breasts are barely adequate; I wear a bra mainly so my clothes will hang properly.

The heavy hand of political correctness has all but killed off the telling of jokes, as most punch lines tend to whack minority groups which are, in today's climate, as inviolate as nuns. Jokes also tend to bring the flow of conversation to a grinding halt. Roger, however, picked up the slack.

"I know it is fashionable to say that I forget a joke seconds after I have heard it, but my problem is that I remember them all. Needless to say most of them do not bear repeating, but I do know one with a slant on fashion. I don't suppose I could beg another mart."

Enough remained in the mason jar for another drink, and Craig poured.

"It seems a farmer wanted to spruce up his farm, so he bought a zebra from a zoo to give the barnyard some swank. On the first day the zebra wandered around introducing herself to the other animals, along the lines of "How do you do. I'm a zebra. What are you and what do you do around here?" An obliging hen explained all about laying eggs and raising chicks. A workhorse, recognizing a distant cousin in the zebra, told her all about pulling a plough, a cart, a hay wain. In turn, a friendly cow explained about raising calves and giving milk. The zebra was delighted with her new home and continued to explore. On turning a corner, she came upon a solidly fenced-in paddock which held what looked like a super cow — large, massive, muscular, with impressive horns and a ring through its nose. Sidling up to the fence the zebra batted her lashes and inquired, "And what do you do around here?"

The bull eyed her for a moment, snorted, and replied, "Just take off those fancy pyjamas and I'll soon show you!""

Again we all laughed obediently. Not surprisingly, I found Roger's joke more amusing, not to say less aggressive, than the one told by Jonathan.

"Your turn, Craig" announced Jonathan with the exaggerated *bonhomie* that only several martinis can induce.

"I'm not much of a *raconteur*," admitted Craig, "but I did hear a definition the other day that amused me. You know you're a redneck when your truck has curtains and your house hasn't."

I laughed from the sheer surprise at hearing Craig tell a joke. The men smiled indulgently. Jonathan, acting like a self-styled master of ceremonies, waved a languid hand in my direction. "You must have a joke, Louise, an amusing story for us."

The only story I wanted to tell was not amusing, and I wanted to relate it in private to Craig, namely that his Aunt Diana was facing surgery. I had hoped to tell him this evening over dinner. This was serious family news, not to be tossed off with a "By the way" as he headed for the shower or took ice from the refrigerator.

I shrugged. "Stand-up comedy has never been my thing, so I'll just borrow a joke my husband used to tell. It dates back to a time of padded shoulders and bobby pins, not to mention open-toed, sling-back pumps. A young man moved from a small city, say Drumondville, to Montreal in order to make good. Some months later a school friend from Drumondville came to Montreal for a visit, and the two young men went out to lunch. The visitor was visibly impressed by his friend's newfound prosperity and asked what he was doing. "Just between you and me I'm a bond salesman," replied the first young man, "but when you get back to Drumondville, please don't tell Mother. She thinks I'm playing piano in a whorehouse.""

While everyone was laughing, I managed to snag Craig's attention long enough to mouth the word "dinner." Roger and Jonathan were on their way to being bombed, and the sooner we ate the sooner I would be able to say goodnight. In my present frame of mind I was not in the mood for company, but I would not be called upon to make much effort.

For once the elevator arrived promptly, and the combined colognes of Roger and Jonathan overwhelmed the residual traces of Chanel, Guerelain, and Rochas. Luckily I have no allergies.

The doorman had a high old time blowing his boy scout whistle, and shortly two taxis pulled up at the curb.

"Johnny, you know the restaurant," said Craig. "Why don't you go with Louise and I'll take Roger." Upon which Craig and Roger climbed neatly into the first cab and sped away.

Jonathan opened the door. "I really should let you get in first, but I think it is more chivalrous of me to clamber over the drive-shaft."

I followed Jonathan into the taxi and managed to close the door. What happened next surprises me every time I think of it. Granted, the drink Craig poured for me was a boilermaker, the kind of belt only a non-drinker will serve. I was angry about having to share Craig with two old queens.

Storm clouds loomed. I was in the mood to drop a couple of depth charges, and I did.

"I'm very pleased to see Craig making new friends like you and Roger," I began in a tone that Walter used to call my Earnest Earnestine voice, a little husky and oh-so-sincere. "I'm frankly worried about my son — and I'll die if you repeat a word of what I'm saying. This conversation is strictly privileged and not to go beyond this cab."

"Why should you be worried about Craig? He seems to be in control of his life. Has he said anything to upset you?"

"That's just it. He hasn't uttered a word, but I know he has something weighing on his mind. Work seems to be going well, and he wants to move to Montreal, as he probably told you. So my gut instinct tells me it's something about his health."

"He looks perfectly sound to me."

In the dim light of the taxi, I could tell Jonathan did not wish to pursue this conversation, but I was relentless.

"What bothers me is that if he had an acceptable illness, say diabetes, or emphysema, or leukaemia, he would probably have told me about it. But there are still some kinds of illness that men are reluctant to confess to their mothers, particularly if they are single men on the cusp of middle age ..." I broke off, confident that I now had Jonathan's full attention.

"Do you mean what I think you mean. That he is —"

"Please!" I cut him off. "Don't jump to conclusions. As I said, I am only guessing — and again I must insist that this conversation is privileged. It's just that it is such a relief to admit to someone how worried I am. Heaven knows, I could be dead wrong — and I hope to God I am. But I've known Craig a long time, and I'm pretty tuned in to his moods."

"Son of a bitch," muttered Jonathan.

"As I said, I'm so glad that Craig has a couple of dependable older friends like you and Roger. And if he and Roger are having a little fling, what's the harm in that? I know Craig is too principled a man ever to put anyone's health in jeopardy. Well, well, is this the restaurant? Once again, Mum's the word."

Jonathan fumbled in his pocket for money. "Oh, no," I said, "let me pay. This is Craig's evening, and I know he wants you and Roger to have a good time."

Jonathan climbed out of the taxi after me and closed the door in a way that suggested he was not pleased. Shameful though it may sound, I felt a surge of elation. I had opened Pandora's box, let the cat out of the bag, torched a bridge or two, and thrown caution to the winds. All in all it was a full agenda for a brief taxi ride, and now it was time to face the music. I could only hope the end justified the means.

Craig and Roger were already seated, Roger on a banquette, Craig facing him on a chair. He rose as we came in and indicated I was to sit beside Roger on the banquette, a more comfortable seat. Instead Jonathan edged past me to claim the banquette for himself.

"Would you prefer the banquette, Louise?" asked Roger.

"No, no, I'll be fine right here," I said placatingly. "I can watch the people coming into the restaurant."

Craig held my chair, Roger beamed at me across the table, and Jonathan looked as though he had just sat on something cold, wet, and malodorous. A waiter who looked like a moon-lighting college student handed menus around and asked if we would like a drink.

"Double gin on the rocks!" said Jonathan after giving the waiter an appraising look.

"A little drop of gineva doesn't sound half bad," said Roger. "I'll have the same."

"Scotch and water, no ice please." I said in turn.

Craig ordered a beer, and we addressed ourselves to the menu. Most Italian menus are reassuring in that they offer few surprises: a couple of pasta entrées, one or two risottos, veal scaloppini, a fish, and at the bottom of the *table d'hôte*, steak. One can usually decide on what to eat before entering the restaurant.

The waiter brought drinks, then took our order, which was easy, as we all chose the veal. Craig asked to see the wine list.

"Louise, do you prefer red or white?"

"Either suits me, certainly with veal. Let the men decide." If God had not struck me with a lightning bolt in the taxi, I presumed He would let me get away with that bit of Betty Boop bullshit.

"Jonathan? Do you have a preference?"

"I think I'll stick with gin."

"Roger?"

"My preference is for red. Most whites these days are too acidic, unless you are prepared to pay three figures. So let's go for a nice, plonky little red."

"Pouring grape on top of all that gin will make you more pissed than you already are." Jonathan spoke to Roger without looking at him.

"Tich, tich. Time for a refresher course at the Gengis Khan Charm School."

Jonathan retreated into silence. For most people, to be silent suggests a certain passivity, a willingness to let others speak. With Jonathan, however, silence became aggression. His rigid spine, crossed hands, brows drawn together suggested he was about to pass sentence on us all.

"I know it's wicked of me to even think this," began Roger, "but at this moment I'd kill for a cigarette."

"Aren't you on the patch?" inquired Craig.

"Yes, and I know I should be strong. But — oh, God — A drag! A drag! My kingdom for a drag!"

"Do shut up about smoking! hissed Jonathan. "I'd kill for a smoke myself, but not with our scoutmaster here." He shot a venomous look at Craig.

"Have a breadstick instead." I offered the basket. "If you've come this far, it does seem a shame to backslide." I flashed a bright, encouraging smile across the table. Jonathan gave me a look that suggested he would not hesitate to shoot me between the eyes.

That smile turned out to be the last one for a while. It vanished from my face as I saw Helen Morrison come into the restaurant with another couple. Considering the hour, I knew she must have put away a couple of drinks. Almost immediately she spotted me and called out a cheery, "Hi, Louise, small world and all like that there."

Trapped, I gave a small, half-hearted wave. By reflex, Roger and Jonathan turned around to see who had spoken. Realizing her gaffe, Helen turned her back on our table and spoke earnestly to the maitre d', who led the party into the second dining room, safely out of range.

But the damage had been done.

"So you know one another." Jonathan spoke quietly, but his expression did not reassure.

It has been observed that the truth will set us free. That may not be entirely correct, but there are occasions when the truth can save a lot of time. "She used to be my sister-in-law. And, yes, she told me what you wanted to charge, a good three hundred dollars more than the estimation you gave me. I wanted to find out whether you were an honest dealer. Evidently you are not."

Craig interrupted. "May I ask what this is all about?"

Before I could reply, the waiter arrived with the wine and the Caesar salads we had all chosen for openers. Once he was out of earshot, I turned to Craig.

"Jonathan is operating a business in defiance of co-op

regulations. When I realized you were probably sleeping with him, I was not pleased. I wanted to find out if he was on the level, so I conspired — don't you love that word — conspired with Helen. She posed as a buyer and expressed interest in Walter's antique decanters, which I had given to Jonathan on consignment. He lied about the price he was asking, meaning I would have ended up with less than half the money earned. Does that answer your question?"

"More than."

Jonathan finished his drink in one swallow. "Somehow I feel I have become *persona non grata* at this table." Pushing brusquely past me, he stood. "I may take a fair sized commission on my sales, but I don't go around accusing people of being HIV-positive without proof. Roger, do you have your key?"

"Yes."

"Then perhaps I'll see you later." With that Jonathan strode from the restaurant.

Roger spoke. "Craig, I have only one question to ask. This seems to be truth time, so answer accordingly. Were you on with Jonathan?"

"Yes."

"When I asked you in Ottawa you said you were just casual acquaintances. Had I known about you two, I would not have slept with you. Jonathan is one of my oldest friends. You lied to me about something I consider important. I don't think I want to eat your food." Roger edged his way from the banquette, no easy feat. "Please excuse me, Louise." He nodded his head in my direction and left.

For a moment Craig and I sat under a bell jar of silence.

"I'm going to move to the banquette," I volunteered. "That way I won't get a crick in my neck talking to you. Now that we have four dinners to eat, we might as well be comfortable."

I edged my way onto the banquette and busied myself with changing the place settings so that I had my own cutlery and napkin.

Craig took a thoughtful sip of wine. "I don't know what you and Jonathan talked about in the cab coming over, but it sounds as though you told him I was HIV-positive."

I, too, paused for a sip of wine, to marshal my forces. "I did not use those initials with that man! If that sounds like a quotation, it's deliberate. What I did suggest is that you are suffering from an unfortunate disease which, at the moment, appears to have no cure. And I'm right."

"And what is this supposed malady?"

"Terminal self-absorption." I paused for a moment to let my words sink in.

"That is a new one. Did you find it on the Internet?"

"No. I diagnosed it by watching you operate. You had hardly crossed the threshold of my new apartment before you were putting the make on my neighbour. Or do I have it wrong?" I took a mouthful of salad.

Craig hesitated a moment. "No, you are right. But you might be interested to know I had a reason."

"Do tell." I reached for a piece of bread and spread it thickly with sweet butter.

"Jonathan has contacts. He can open doors for me, or could before you tossed him overboard."

"Craig, why do artists have agents, or galleries? So they won't have to sleep with the neighbours in order to hustle their work. Is that why you put out for Roger?"

"I suppose it is. I know you disapprove, Louise. That is your right. What you don't realize is that a great deal more than just talent goes into making a career. You have to have breaks, timing, contacts, and luck. I have plans. And if accommodating a couple of men who could hardly be called choirboys is part of the deal, so be it. I'm sorry you don't approve, but there it is."

"There is a rude word for people who sell themselves for gain, financial or otherwise, which I will refrain from using. Aside from the sheer sleaziness of hustling older men for personal advancement, I have recently learned that Jonathan was fully prepared to cheat me on a transaction. I also have ample cause to suspect he took shocking advantage of the previous owner of my apartment. I believe he stole from her, only there is no way I can prove it. He is a dishonest man, a foul weather friend; he lives directly across the hall from me; you are my son; and I do not want you involved with him in any way, shape or form. *Voilà tout!*"

"This is not like you, Louise. I have always admired you for not interfering in my life. But this time you've really balled things up."

I reached for the bottle and refilled my glass. "I'm not so sure about that. I think you've done a pretty good job of compromising us both. This has been a double date that will live in infamy. I am reminded of that stand-up comedy line: 'This morning I woke up in a strange bed — mine!' You probably won't believe this; but, for what it's worth, I really do not care that Jonathan is a man. There are only two sexes, and most of us choose one or the other. But he is my neighbour, and he is bad news. This may surprise you, but I'm sorry you've fallen afoul of Roger. I like him. I question his judgement in having Jonathan as a friend, but I still like him."

Craig looked directly into my eyes. "You do not want to face reality. You want the skies to be blue and the little birds to go tweet, tweet, tweet. It comes from retiring to that brackish backwater for so many years."

"That is nonsense. Reality is for people who can't face drugs, and I can't even inhale tobacco. However we are going around in circles, and I would like to declare a truce. I had hoped to see you alone tonight because I have some serious family news."

The arrival of our veal caused an interruption. Craig explained to the waiter that the others had been called away unexpectedly and asked him to leave the extra dinners.

Craig is lean, but he can put away the foodstuffs. Once we had been served, I told him about Diana. I knew Craig to be very attached to his aunt, who had been good to him as a child. He promised to visit her tomorrow.

"I realize you must be upset about Aunt Diana," he concluded, "but that does not excuse your behaving like an out-of-control harpie."

"Weren't the Harpies Greek? Perhaps, considering your present lifestyle, you should learn more about Trojans."

"Jesus, Louise, you do have a mouth. Why don't you use it to finish your dinner."

Having both scored a point, we subsided into silence. After so much high drama, we both felt deflated. An adrenaline high wears off. We also understood that our relationship would never again be the same. I had succeeded in discrediting Jonathan, but at what cost to Craig and me remained to be seen. Oddly enough, in no way did I regret my outrageous behaviour. I do not think for a second that family ties excuse bad behaviour, and I honestly believed Craig had behaved atrociously. If he could not make it as a painter without networking in bed, then he should find some other line of endeavour. His behaviour called my success or failure as parent into question. My self-esteem was on the line. And I discovered I was quite prepared to deal from the bottom of the deck in order to flush the enemy.

I ate my dinner; Craig ate two; and the fourth went back untasted. With a minimum of talk Craig paid the bill, and we took a taxi back to Queen's Court. After a perfunctory goodnight we went to our respective rooms, having moved way beyond casual conversation, at least for the moment. The following morning Craig went to visit Diana on his way to the airport. He flew to Toronto for a few days, then back to the West Coast. His plan to move to Montreal went on hold. He did not kiss me goodbye.

ൟ

The following morning I called Sloane, Drummond, Gladstone and Crossen, an accounting firm with offices in the Sun Life building, and asked for an appointment with Derek Sloane. I knew he was on the board of directors for Queen's Court, and I wanted to have what my mother used to call "a little talk." The secretary informed me she had a cancellation for eleven-thirty that morning, making the announcement in a tone suggesting she was conferring a great favour. Suitably and soberly dressed, medium heels, skirt to the knee, touches of gold at wrist and throat, I presented myself at the reception desk where a perky receptionist, hair in a ponytail, asked me to take a seat. I avoided the leather armchair, which looked treacherously deep, in favour of a prim settee behind a low table on which lay business magazines in neat, parallel rows.

They did not look tempting. I was incurious about the hundred best small companies in Canada or the fifty most promising sales managers in Ontario. Usually I carry a book for just such emergencies, but my tasteful handbag was too small to conceal a fat paperback.

Derek Sloane kept me waiting ten minutes, more I suspect from gamesmanship than pressures of work. In his middle years, he wore the smooth, glossy look of someone who works out, eats well, vacations in Florida, and has an alternate source of income. He greeted my outstretched palm with both hands.

"Good morning, Mrs. Bingham," he began, flashing a high-maintenance smile, "sorry to keep you waiting. Won't you step into my office?"

I entered a masculine snuggery of dark wood, oriental rugs, gilt-framed pictures, leather chairs, and a cluster of large potted plants. Seated on the opposite side of a broad desk, while the sleek Mr. Sloane lounged in his leather chair, I was reminded of being sent to the principal's office in school; however, on this occasion, I was the one with a grievance.

"Now, Mrs. Bingham, what can I do for you? I hope you are settling into Queen's Court quite comfortably."

"More or less. And it is precisely concerning Queen's Court that I am here. According to the regulations laid down for the co-op, no resident is allowed to operate a business on the premises."

"That is correct."

"Well, Mr. Sloane, my neighbour directly across the hall is doing precisely that."

"Precisely what?" repeated Derek Sloane as though I had postulated an arcane and impenetrable proposition.

"My neighbour, Jonathan Barclay, is running an antiques business out of his apartment, in contravention of co-op regulations."

"Oh, that." Derek Sloane gave me the condescending smile suitable for a sulky ten year-old. "He's been doing that for years, sort of a cottage industry. As a matter of fact, Mrs. Bingham," Derek Sloane leaned forward to rest his arms comfortably on the desk, "at one time or another almost all the residents of Queen's Court have had dealings with him, including my wife. Often, when people move out, they give him things on consignment. It is a bit under-the-table, I agree; but he's never bothered anybody, so we just look the other way."

I leaned forward, resting my right hand on the edge of the desk. "I am not prepared to look the other way. Further- more, over the last few days I have discovered that he is dishonest."

The smile faded. Derek Sloane sat upright. "How so?"

Briefly I explained about enlisting Helen Morrison to make an offer on my decanters. "I am quite prepared to believe that I am not the first person he has attempted to scam. How many residents of Queen's Court do you suppose have been bilked?"

Derek Sloane permitted a frown to crease his perfect forehead. "Good question. What do you intend to do?"

"What do I intend to do? I don't think it is up to me. I am not on the board of directors. The question is what you intend to do. Unless you want me to bring up the subject at the next general meeting, which is next month, I believe."

As I sat in that expensive armchair in that opulent office, I experienced a gestalt, a synapse, a sudden realization that I did not intend to go on living in Queen's Court. For me the place was jinxed. I had not been there long enough to send down roots, and the apartment had brought me nothing but grief.

Derek Sloane rubbed his hands together, miming washing, before answering. "I had not intended to do anything, unless you absolutely insist. You are perfectly within your right to complain. The rules are the rules. But we have lived with the status quo for some time now. Is it really necessary to rock the boat?"

I hesitated before answering, an idea only half formed beginning to take shape. "I have a suggestion, more of an offer, really. I have good reason to believe that Mr. Barclay has in his possession china and silver belonging to the former owner of my unit, Mrs. Phyllis Donaldson. If Mr. Barclay will agree to return these items to Beatrice Lane, Mrs. Donaldson's niece, then I will agree not to pursue the matter further."

Derek Sloane leaned back in his chair, fingers pressed together supporting his chin. "That seems like a fair offer. I'm sure I speak for the other directors when I say we would prefer not to turn this incident into an issue."

I nodded. "I would prefer you to deal with Mr. Barclay directly. Not surprisingly, we are not on good terms at the moment. I will be in touch with Mrs. Lane to see if he has complied." I stood. "I guess that about covers it, Mr. Sloane. Thanks for seeing me on such short notice."

Derek Sloane crossed the oriental to open the door. I inclined my head. We did not shake hands. And that was the end of the interview.

꙾

I took myself out for a bite of lunch and a period of reflection. Life is never tidy, but at times it becomes more untidy than one would wish. On the plus side I had driven a wedge between Craig and Jonathan; I had arranged for Phyllis Donaldson's heirlooms to be restored to her niece; and I had called Jonathan's credibility into question with a member of the board of directors.

But there were minus factors to consider. The most looming was my damaged relationship with my only son. We have never before had a major falling out. I was sorry we had, but not sorry enough to regret the steps I had taken.

My nose myself I painted white
Because, you see, I'm always right.

Right, wrong, or both at once, I had to live first of all with myself. I hoped the situation would blow over. Time is supposed to be a great healer, and I will just have to wait this one out.

In the meantime I intended to push ahead with my sudden decision to leave Queen's Court. On quiet reflection, it seemed the best way to go. Since I moved into the apartment, I had watched Sean reenter and leave my life, I had fallen out with the neighbour, I had discovered things about my son I would have preferred not to know, and I had learned Diana was seriously ill. The apartment was not to blame, but the rooms were still dank with bad news.

Furthermore, I had a place to go. I would move into the vacant apartment in Diana's building, pay her rent, and play it one day at a time. Possibly I had been too hasty in buying a flat, the urge for something permanent after leaving my home in Victoria clouding my judgement. I knew I would have no difficulty in reselling my co-op. The housing market was hot at the moment, and vacancy rates were near zero.

As I signalled for the cheque, I realized I had not minded eating lunch alone. Perhaps it was just as well, as it looked as though I would be spending a good deal of time in my own company from now on. A widow my age generally lunches with other women or gay men, and I was rather off gay men at the moment. No doubt this would pass. And the city teemed with people I had yet to meet. Somehow I would manage, and, if I failed, the fault would be mine alone.

Envoi

iana emerged from surgery into a remarkably fast recovery. She is officially in remission. The lingering effect of her ordeal is that she is now on the verge of becoming an old lady. Gone are the inexhaustible energy, the drive to improve the world, the conviction that every moment not spent on promoting a worthy cause is a moment wasted. She is now content to live out her life in sepia tones, all of which means she does not intrude upon my life the way I had initially feared. I live quite comfortably at Three Forest Road in the flat I now rent from Diana. It lacks the charm of Queen's Court, but it is mercifully free of associations. Beryl Burke managed to sell my apartment for more than I had paid. As a token of gratitude, I gave her the pair of conten-

tious decanters which she had admired. Now I won't have
them around to remind me of past unpleasantness.

Craig moved east to Toronto, possibly a better location for
a unilingual artist than French Montreal. We are back on
good terms, and he sleeps in the alcove off the living room
whenever he comes to Montreal, which is not often. Toronto
is closer than Vancouver, granted, but I see no more of him
now than when I lived in Victoria. He continues to paint,
and his career appears to be going well. I no longer probe
too deeply.

Sean put his possessions into storage and went off to England
to work on his book. He telephoned from the airport while
waiting for his flight. He also promised to send me an address
as soon as he was settled, and urged me to come for a visit.
London is out of the question because of his budget, but he
spoke of Bath, a city I would love to explore.

My brother Christopher has invited me to visit him in
Sarasota, and Helen Morrison wants me to go on a long
cruise around the Mediterranean. I might also get off my
backside and find a volunteer job, not for self-justification
but stimulation. Something positive, like fostering literacy
or teaching English to immigrants, a.k.a. New Canadians.

Jonathan returned the china and silver to Beatrice Lane,
for reasons he naturally did not explain to me; and I did
not pursue the matter further. For all I know, he is still
bilking the residents of Queen's Court, but he is no longer
my problem. I saw him once on Sherbrooke Street, after I

had moved. After catching sight of me he became suddenly very absorbed in a shop window until I had safely passed him by. *Sic transit*.

A few days before I was to move out of Queen's Court, I received a call from the moving company which had packed and shipped me east. The two missing boxes had turned up in a warehouse outside Toronto, and could they be delivered tomorrow. I did not bother to unpack them until I was settling into Three Forest Road. Pleased though I was to have a number of things that reminded me of Walter, I was truly delighted to recover my two postcard portraits of Keats and Lorca. They could not replace the men who had moved out of my orbit, but nor were they about to bring me any grief.

At this point in my life that struck me as a pretty good trade-off. Not that I am indulging in a kind of defiant optimism, but I am all grown up and should be able to cope. Besides, being grown up means being able to say no to Jell-O salads, Spandex, and Christmas sing-a-longs.

What more could I want?